THE WIZARD KNIGHT COMPANION

A LEXICON FOR GENE WOLFE'S
THE KNIGHT and *THE WIZARD*

MICHAEL ANDRE-DRIUSSI

with a foreword by
GENE WOLFE

SIRIUS FICTION
Albany, California

Copyright © 2009 by Michael Andre-Driussi

All rights reserved. No part of this book may be reproduced in any form without written permission from the publisher.

Book and cover design by Nicole Hayward Design.

Cover art: Large coat of arms © David Crooks/iStock. Cosmology illustration, page 4: Palm tree © Cheryl Savala/iStock; Dancing Elf © Natasha Graham; Dragon © Sunil Aggarwal/iStock.

First edition: 2009

Hardcover ISBN: 978-0-9642795-2-0
Paperback ISBN: 978-0-9642795-3-7

Printed in the United States of America.

Sirius Fiction
P.O. Box 6248
Albany, CA 94706

CONTENTS

Foreword by Gene Wolfe — vii

Map of Celidon — x

Detail Map of Northern and Central Celidon — x

Introduction — 1

Cosmology — 4

THE WIZARD KNIGHT COMPANION — 5

The Wizard Knight Synopsis — 109

Bibliography — 120

FOREWORD

Gene Wolfe

Michael Andre-Driussi knows me far better than I know myself. When I cannot find something in the refrigerator, for example, I email MAD pleasantly: "Dear Michael, How are you? How are your wife and kids? Last night I bought a small box of cookies. (The black kind with white icing inside.) I hid them in the refrigerator so well I cannot find them tonight. Any help that you can provide will be greatly appreciated. Faithfully, Gene Wolfe PS. Do not say the vegetable drawer. I have looked there. Do not say the freezer either."

Michael replies: "Dear Gene: This reminds me of the well-known instance in *The Wizard Knight* in which you concealed Able's last name until he closed his letter to his brother. That is to say, the answer was not obvious, yet the place of concealment was obvious. Just so in this instance: your wife has found your cookies and eaten them. Sincerely yours, Michael"

That exchange is only too typical. It is well-known to all my readers that I often forget characters and plot lines while writing.

And afterward.

Fortunately, MAD has addressed this by writing this book. You will find all that stuff right here. Suppose, for example that I recall Lord Beel and his daughter (whatever her name was). I desire to use them in a new story laid "in the same universe," as editors say, as *The Wizard*. (or *The Knight*.) We could call it *An Update from Mythgarthr: Part III*.

I open this book at random: "COLDCLIFF Beel's father's castle (I, chap. 48, 301) now belonging to Beel's brother (I, chap. 54, 337)." Now the whole thing becomes simplicity itself. The central character will be Lord Beel. The thing he wants (sometimes called the McGuffin) is the castle of Coldcliff. He will journey to Coldcliff, accompanied by his daughter whatshername, that prince she married, and half a dozen lady giants. Let us begin.

"Father dear," (his daughter will say plaintively) "you know you can't possibly gain Coldcliff without you murder my uncle whatshisname." (The copyeditor will fix up her diction, never fear.) "Surely you wood never stain the family escutcheon with your brother's blood. Can't you get somebody else to do it?"

"Hardly practical, my deer." (The spelling, too.) Beel smiles in superior and highly annoying fashion.

"I could arrange things so that Svon is seated next to him at dinner, Daddy. Svon can be perfectly infuriating, and he's a fine swordsman. The carving knife will be child's play to him."

"But what if my brother whatshisname should kill Prince Svon?"

"Well, easy come, easy go. If that should happen we could offer your brother whatshisname a lap dance by one of my giantesses. A lapdancing giantess should squash just about anybody."

Her father smiled again, it was not only highly annoying but smug. "I have saved my noble brother from being squashed, my deer. I have told him the king has need of him."

"He does?"

"Not as far as I know, but farther. I have sent him to the Mountain of Fire."

"Wow! That's a long way. Why not Thortower?"

"Because he could probably find it. I think this book tells you more or less where it is."

"It tells you where the Mountain of Fire is, too, Daddy."

"Yes, but it's much farther away. Besides, I told him the king was down inside."

"I . . . see."

"Don't look at me like that, deer. Since nobody knows who succeeded King Arnthor, it may well be true. And of course after my dear brother sees the king down there, he will have to come back to Kingsdoom."

"Why not here, Daddy?"

"Because the book doesn't tell you where this McGuffin is, of course. We, however, are here. Possession is nine points of the law."

"Pretty soon me and Prince Whosis will go back to Whatchamaycallit."

"Jotunland, deer."

"Jotunhome. Read the book, Daddy."

"An excellent suggestion."

You see? Right there I have my story in a nutshell, just by peeking in here. Tie a knot in the plot, add a hundred pages of characterization, and I'd have a new novel. I'm telling you, this book is a gold mine!

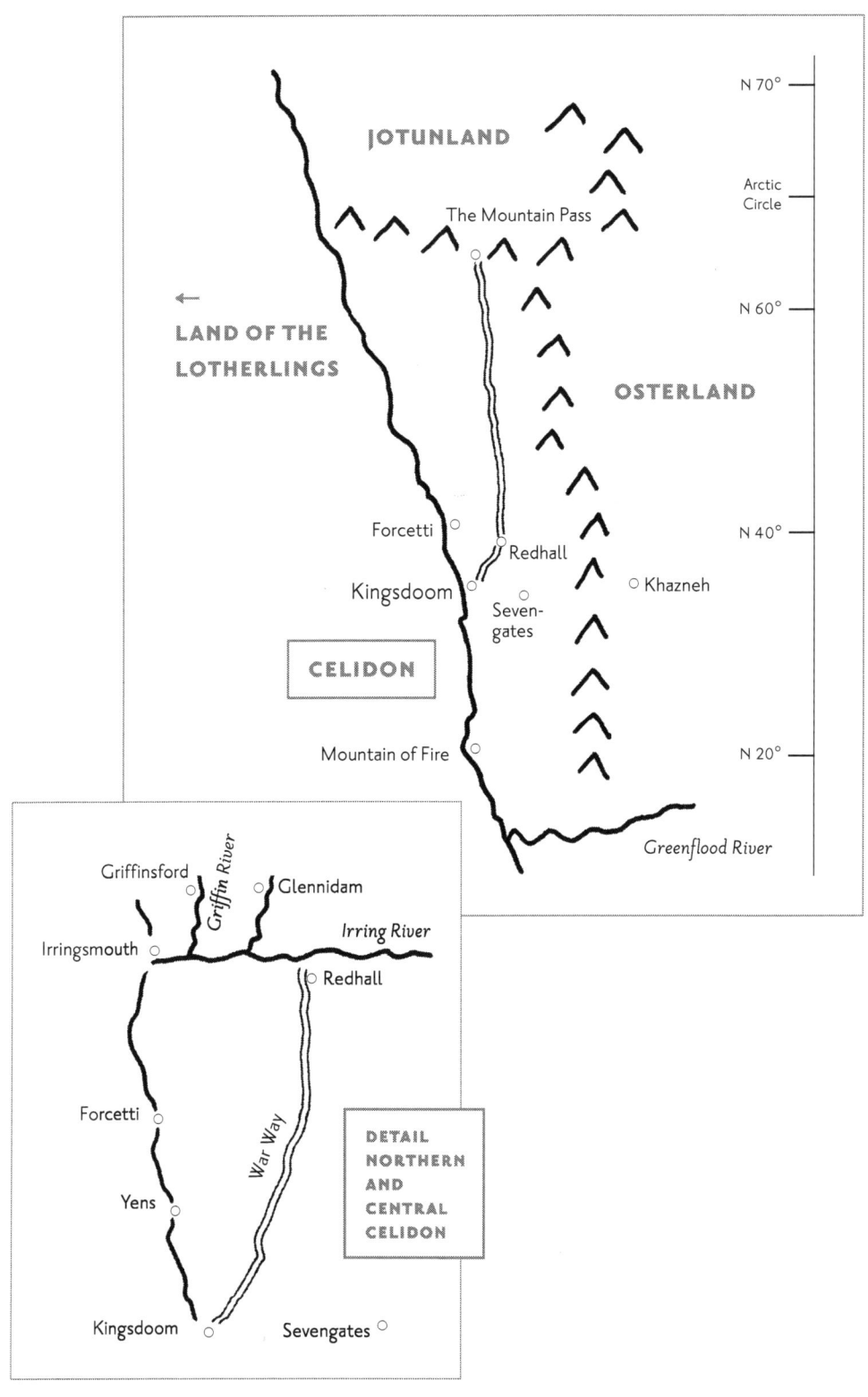

INTRODUCTION

"We have *The Book of the New Sun*," said Michael Straight in cold indignation, "and they give us a movie of *The Golden Compass*."

"Yeah!" said James Wynn and I. We would've spit, too, but there were women and children around.

We were at a waterfront restaurant in Seattle, along with Mrs. Wynn, and my wife and my two kids. It was June 16, 2007, about an hour before Gene Wolfe's induction into the Science Fiction Hall of Fame, a day in which I had decided to write this book, but I didn't bother to mention that at the time.

The situation was complicated by the fact that I already owed another book, the proposed *Gate of Horn, Book of Silk*, and I'd owed it for years. My thinking was that I'd first do a quick and easy second edition of *Lexicon Urthus*, then I'd buckle down and do the three-sevenths of the work remaining on *Gate*. But at breakfast it came to me that *Gate* was already years late, so another year or two wouldn't matter. And sales of *The Wizard Knight* were strong in Europe as well as America, so why not write a book about that while it was relatively fresh? It should be fairly quick and easy: after all, I was long familiar with Norse mythology, and I knew a bit of Arthuriana.

Well, it turned out to be not quite that easy.

I never really know what my own reading is until I start sharing notes with other readers. That's the first shock, seeing where my own unsuspected assumptions have led me astray. As a result everything is tested, checked. For example, I was so sure that the character Lothur was playing the role of Norse Loki (and perhaps even Lucifer!) that I failed to trace the name to Odin's least famous brother. In another, the shaggy ponies of the Lothurlings convinced me so thoroughly of their Mongolian nature that I assumed the character He Who Smiles had led his group across land from the East, just as the Mongols had swept to the edge of Europe from the East. Because the Mongols had terrible luck with overseas invasions, having tried to invade Japan twice across a relatively narrow stretch of water, I couldn't imagine the Lothurlings making an ocean crossing. This caused several headaches in the map-making process until I was ready to accept the rather obvious fact that they seem to have come across the Western water more in the style of Cortez. The Mongolian linkage to both the Lothurlings (with their Mongolian ponies) and the Osterlings (with their Mongolian "caans") caused me to periodically confuse the two groups.

Even my sense of Celidon having a Norse culture proved to be less than accurate. After all, the pagan Scandinavians had sacred groves, temples, and priests. They had wooden idols and even shrine wagons that brought the blessings of agricultural gods to distant farms. None of this is evident in Celidon: there are no priests, no temples, no statues, and no shrines. The primary belief system seems to be in ghosts, and there may be a rudimentary nature cult worshiping Aelf at Glennidam. In short it is the landscape of fairy tale, where raiding giants, trollish Osterlings, and shadowy Aelf are close, while dragons and gods are equally distant and feared. As such it is closer to pre-Norse, or proto-Norse.

Trying to establish the timelines, along with the related question of the relationship between Mrs. Ormsby and Mag ("serial mom or clone moms?"), opened another can of worms.

Then there is my wild suspicion that Gene Wolfe chose "Ormsby" because the noted Gene Wolfe scholar Peter Wright teaches at a university in Ormskirk, the site of such rich Orm lore.

So there we were, three unelected representatives of Wolfe-fandom, who had flown in from different states to be there in the celebration of Our Guy. I looked across the River Gyoll up toward the Old Citadel on the hill, where we would be going soon. A few words cannot convey the headiness of that day or the personal tragedies to come later in that season.

But you have something else on your mind, something you want to say that is as much a reflex as if the doctor's hammer had just tapped you on the knee. Oracular or gnomic, with great delight you say to me: "Oreos."

I nod and smile, so happy to share notes. "Yes, I know what you mean," I say. "But that's just the first impression, isn't it? I mean, after some consideration, I think they must be Hydroxes, really."

Thanks to the following:
Dan'l Danehy-Oakes, who read through the first draft and offered valuable insights.
Scott Wowra, who found glosses for a large number of names that I could not find.
Nigel Price, for valuable leads.
Roy C. Lackey, who surprised me by putting in a tremendous amount of work when I had thought to spare him this time.

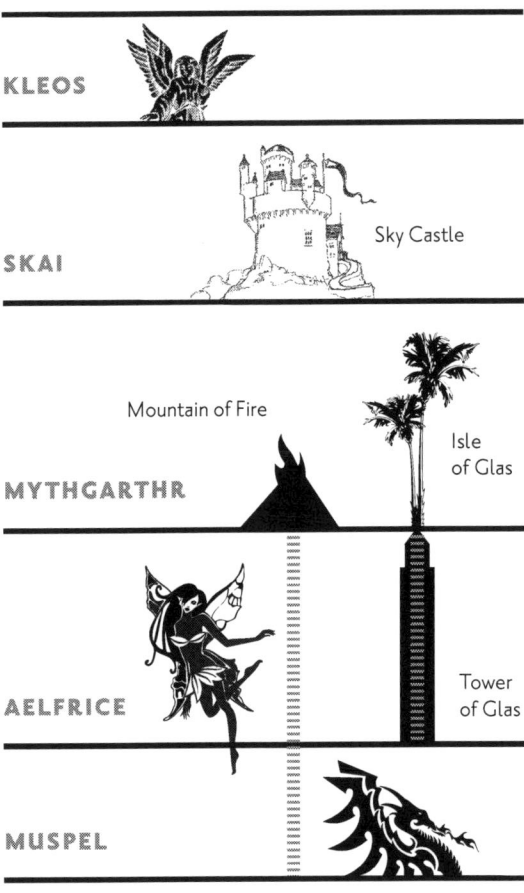

COSMOLOGY

ABLE name given to narrator by Parka, who dubs him Able of the High Heart (see THREE HEARTS AND THREE LIONS). (Also the name of Bold Berthold's brother "whom Disiri switched for me" [II, glossary], for whom see REAL ABLE.) His bow is made of spiny orange and has a magic string given to him by Parka (see BOWSTRING SPIRITS). His first weapon is the strange mace Sword Breaker and he later wins the mythic sword Eterne. Able guesses that Disiri aged him ten years in one night, but Garsecg thinks it was less (I, chap. 25, 162). Able hears both of his names in the wind (I, chap. 67, 412). Able seems a bit like Don Quixote, but he is actually a lot more like Tom O'Bedlam (see both). In Skai he is known as Drakoritter, and among the Lothurlings he is Scatter of the Dragon's Blood. See also ORMSBY, ARTHUR.

Able as tool.
- Disiri, Queen of the Moss Aelf, wants Able to deliver message to Arnthor.

- Garsecg, King of the Sea Aelf, wants Able to kill Kulili.
- Baki, the Fire Aelf, wants Able to lead Aelfrice against Setr, King of the Fire Aelf (II, chap. 11, 114).
- Gilling, King of the Jotun, wants Able to conquer Celidon for him.
- Escan, Arnthor's Earl Marshal, wants Able to take him to Aelfrice.

Able's message is unknown to Able until he starts giving it (II, chap. 33, 396). Arnthor interrupts him from delivering all the parts (398). After being chained in the dungeon, he is visited by Arnthor and he tells him the rest—that Arnthor is a tyrant (II, chap. 35, 417). *Onomastics:* obviously the name is an indicator of ability, but it also has a haunting link to Abel, the younger brother of Cain.

AEGRI'S ISLE a place the giants took by piling dirt to overreach the walls (II, chap. 17, 200).
Myth: close to the Norse Ægir (sea, sea-giant), the god of the sea, whose wife is RAN. In several name lists, Ægir is given as the name of a giant.
Onomastics: the Latin word *aegri* means "sick man."

AELF [alf] the people of the fifth world, made by Kulili (I, glossary; I, chap. 1, 22). There are many different types, including Earth Aelf (the Bodachan, led by King Brunman), Fire Aelf (the Salamanders, formerly led by King Weland, then by Setr), Ice Aelf (led by King Ycer), Moss Aelf (the Skogsalfar, led by Queen Disiri), and Sea Aelf (the Kelpies, led by King Garsecg).

Most of the Aelf were directly made by Kulili. Aelf children are born, but very rarely, such that when they arrive they become king or queen (II, chap. 22, 265). The text tells us that Disiri had a childhood in Aelfrice. Thus she is a second generation Aelf and presumably Moss Queen for that reason.

AELF LETTERS there are three examples given of Aelf characters (I, chap. 68, 419).

Sound	*Name*
K	Kantel
A	Ahlaw
L	Llo

AELF SWORD the weapon fated to kill the Black Caan, which was worn by the old Caan the day his six sons were born. He gave it to the Black Tijanamir, who locked it away.

When Able is in the dungeon of Thortower, Uri steals the sword and gives it to him (II, chap. 34, 407). It is Ice Aelf work (408), and it is thirsty for blood (II, chap. 36, 432). It glows at times, brightest when Arnthor gets it (II, chap. 39, 468).

AELFRICE the fifth world, under Mythgarthr (I, chap. 1, 20). It was Kulili's world first, but after she created the Aelf, they overran the place. See COSMOLOGY.
Myth: (Norse) Alfheim, home of the light elves.

AGR Marder's marshal (I, chap. 32, 198).
Onomastics: Greek *agros* and Latin *agr-*, meaning "field" and having to do with agriculture.

ALBRECHT see NAMES ON THE WIND.

ALCA a slave of Logi (II, chap. 17, 195), probably one of the two sleeping on the hearth (191). Later one of Svon's slaves (II, chap. 23, 277), one of the two women (II, chap. 21, 251). She was paired to a slave named Sceef (277).
Onomastics: (Icelandic) auk, a type of bird.

ALVIT one of the shield-maidens who ride for the Valfather (II, chap. 19, 225). The third Valkyrie to try and catch falling Able, she carried him to Skai (I, chap. 69, 429). She had been a princess and died a virgin, "facing death with dauntless courage" (II, chap. 19, 225).
Myth: (Norse) Hervör alvitr, the daughter of King Hlodver, sometime wife

of Volund (the legendary smith—see WELAND), and a Valkyrie. Orchard writes that *alvitr* is an Old Norse word meaning "all-wise" or "strange creature."

AMABEL the woman who saved Payn when his mother died (II, glossary; II, chap. 36, 431). Her husband is Hrolfr (431).
Onomastics: Latin name meaning "beautiful, loving."

ANGR a giantess of Winter and Old Night, the mother of Angrboda and the Angrborn (I, chap. 61, 376).

ANGRBODA a giantess, daughter of Angr, who wasn't banished from Skai (II, chap. 24, 293-94). She is Lothur's wife, and she attacks all who come near.
Myth: (Norse) "harm-bidder," giantess wife of god Loki, and mother of Fenrir.

ANGRBORN the giants who were forced out of Skai, all descended from a famous giantess named Angr (I, chap. 2, 28). The giants of the ice country (Jotunland).

ARN one of Garvaon's archers (II, chap. 16, 183).
Onomastics: (Swedish) eagle.

ARNTHOR the King of Celidon, his picture is on the coin Ravd gives to Able (I, chap. 4, 43). Disiri gives Able a message for him. His father was Uthor, a human king, and his mother was an unnamed water dragon of Muspel. The youngest of three, his brother is Setr, his sister is Morcaine.
Onomastics: (Norse) Thor the Eagle.
Arthuriana: Arnthor's role is that of a tyrannical Arthur, whose name can be traced to Celtic Artus, "bear."

ATL one of Thunrolf's servants (I, glossary only).
Myth: (Norse) close to Atli, mythic name for a King of the Huns (perhaps based upon Attila).

AUD Thunrolf's steward, who meets Able, Thunrolf, and Pouk when they come up out of the Mountain of Fire (I, chap. 31, 192). Vix is also there.
Myth: (Norse) mythic name "wealth" (son of Nott, "night").

BAHART youngest of the Celidon dukes (II, chap. 39, 465). He survived the River Battle (II, chap. 40, 473) and thus might have become the new king.
Onomastics: possibly from the Arabic *baharat*, "spice," from *bahar*, "black pepper."

BAKI a Fire Aelf girl whom Able meets at the Tower of Glas (I, chap. 23, 149). She is a khimaira at the time. She and Uri say they are his slaves. Baki is the one who renounces Setr. After Marder's knights beat Able, Baki heals him with her blood (I, chap. 33, 206). Soon after Able returns from Skai, Baki is wounded and near death. She claims to have been caught by a giant when she and Uri scattered the mules (II, chap. 4, 51). Able refuses to heal her, having Toug do it (II, chap. 4, 43). Baki would thus have reason to strike Gilling to protect Toug, as Able must think (II, chap. 13, 149). A Fire Aelf posed as a giantess just before the strike was made against Gilling: was it Uri or Baki?

Onomastics: (Hebrew) "expert." There is also a Turkish author of this name, famous for advocating hedonism (wine and women).

BALDIG one of the peasants who used to live in Griffinsford, where his house was across from Uld's (I, chap. 3, 34). Schildstarr picked him up and ripped his arms off (I, chap. 2, 29).
Onomastics: (German) "early" or "quick, speedy."

BALYE a Redhall man-at-arms who bested Able with quarterstaff (II, chap. 27, 338).
Myth: (Norse) close to Baleyg, meaning "flame-eye," a name for Odin.

BARONS the lowest level of nobility, the ruler of a barony. From the French title meaning "military leader." Barons in the text include Beel, Colle, Dandum, Leifr (?), Obr, Olof, and Thunrolf.

BATTLE OF FIVE FATES the battle of King Arnthor versus the Osterlings (II, chap. 11, 127; II, chap. 37, 442–43). Woddet was present. The Golden Caan was also present, with his elephants. The old Caan had six heirs: the Red Tijanamir, the Brown Tijanamir, the White Tijanamir, the Gold Tijanamir, the Blue Tijanamir, and the Black Tijanamir. The old Caan died, and so did the first five heirs, leaving the last one to become the Black Caan.

BATTLE WITCH Garvaon's sword (I, chap. 55, 341).

BATTLEMAID Ravd's sword (I, chap. 4, 42). Broken Battlemaid turns up at the outlaw cave (I, chap. 14, 100).

BEAW one of Garvaon's men-at-arms (I, chap. 58, 357).
Onomastics: Beaw or Beow, a name occurring in the genealogies of Anglo-Saxon kings, thought by some to be a pagan fertility god (Beow = Old English "barley").

BEEL the baron Arnthor sent to Jotunland (I, chap. 47, 294). Able meets him, finding him to be a middle-aged man so short one notices even when he is seated (I, chap. 48, 296). He spent his boyhood in a peasant's house, his nurse's, outside Coldcliff castle (I, chap. 48, 301). His arms are quartered lamiae and lilacs (II, chap. 12, 138). This design suggests a merger of two houses, one previously possessing an emblem of a lamia and the other with that of a lilac. (Note that the Lady is associated with lilacs.) He has served the throne for 25 years (I, chap. 54, 338). His daughter is Idnn. He is something of a magic user, casting a spell of divination at the mountain pass.

Onomastics: Aramaic name Be'el, related to the Hebrew Ba'al, meaning "lord, master." Beelzebub means "lord of the house."

Commentary: Baron Beel is the grandson of King Pholsung and the cousin of King Arnthor. His desire to achieve higher status, if only through his daughter Idnn, is such that he is willing to marry her off to Gilling, King of the Giants.

BELOS one of two Sea Aelf who come to Able after the halbert contest, trying to bring him to the princess Morcaine (II, chap. 30, 370).

Onomastics: Wistan translates it as "warlike" (which may mean it derives from Latin *bello*, to wage war).

Myth: (Greek) grandson of Epaphos, father of Danaos and Aigyptos.

BEN the narrator's brother back in America (I, glossary) whom he sees sitting by the campfire after battle (I, chap. 1, 19), on the day of the River Battle. Sometimes he writes directly to Ben: "The truth, Ben, is that I had already decided" (II, chap. 37, 448); "You know what I was tempted to say, Ben" (II, chap. 38, 452); "Far less than you, Ben" (II, chap. 38, 457).

Some statements to Ben are more ambiguous, for example, "Where you are, people kill people all the time just like they do here" (I, chap. 14, 96). At first this seems to be comparing America to Mythgarthr, but later revelations make it more likely that it is comparing Mythgarthr (where Ben is) to Aelfrice (where Able is).

After Able heals Bold Berthold's eyes, when he looks through the magic helm, he sees that Berthold is Ben. And thus Ben is in Mythgarthr (II, chap. 40, 476).

Still, the question remains as to the location of Ben when he receives the letter from Art. If Ben were really in Mythgarthr, then it would not make sense for Art to write the following lines: "What was hard was making you see them. Remember that the Osterlings had long teeth and starved faces, and the Angrborn stunk. Remember that Disiri was a shapechanger, and all her shapes were beautiful" (I, glossary end). Since Able watches Bold Berthold's later career as a giant slayer, he would not have to fret about describing giants to him unless Ben was not there for long. That is, Ben is not Bold Berthold. This builds a strong case that Ben snapped back to America after Able left Mythgarthr for Aelfrice, so that Ben only experienced a strange "dream" of being by the campfire with knights and his brother.
Onomastics: Hebrew word for "son."

BERGELMIR one of Ymir's body parts that lived after he was dismembered by the Overcyns (II, chap. 17, 188); the first king of Jotunland, ancestor of Gilling (II, chap. 14, 156). The kings of the giants descend from him.
Myth: (Norse) the giant who survived the flood of blood from slaughtered Ymir.

BERTHOLD for Berthold the Black, see BLACK BERTHOLD. For Berthold the Bold, see BOLD BERTHOLD.

BITERGARM a giant randomly selected to fight the knights in Gilling's hall (II, chap. 12, 137). (The other was Skoel.) He later saw the party of humans again, just after they had buried Garvaon (II, chap. 27, 329).
Onomastics: bitr means bitter, and Garm is the name of a famous hell hound, so perhaps "bitter hellhound."

BLACK BERTHOLD father of Bold Berthold and the real Able. The leader of Griffinsford, he was noted for his great strength. Mag tells

Able she once saw him wrestle a bull and hold it down (II, chap. 38, 458). When the village was under attack by forces from lower levels, Black Berthold built an altar to the Overcyns, which makes him a religious figure or perhaps a prophet whose teachings didn't take (II, chap. 22, 264).

Mag uses the form Berthold the Black (II, chap. 22, 263), whereas Bold Berthold uses Black Berthold (II, chap. 38, 458).

Commentary: it seems likely Black Berthold was a smith. There is the name *Black*, which can signify swarthy skin and/or black hair, but is also part of blacksmith. There is his great strength—he could wrestle a bull down. Though strength alone may not be sufficient evidence in another book, the text makes it particularly clear that smiths are very strong.

There is evidence of a basic mirroring between Art in America and the real Able in Celidon, such that if Mr. Ormsby was in "hardware," then Black Berthold must be in the local equivalent, which would be village blacksmith.

Finally, Black Berthold was the leader of his village. It would be very significant if he were also a blacksmith, because Aelfrice has a very special esteem for blacksmith leaders. This would tie into the whole Weland complex: it makes sense that the wizard knight Sir Able would be the son of a smith.

BLACK CAAN the Caan seeking vengeance for the raids from Celidon (II, chap. 35, 413), the raids that Woddet took part in (II, chap. 11, 126). So presumably the Black Caan hopes to avenge the looting of Khazneh and the killing of his brothers at the Battle of Five Fates. He is the heir of the old Caan who was killed in the surprise attack (launched when Celidon's north border with the giants was secured, so that all forces could sweep east). The Osterlings rally around the Black Caan and take the passes (413).

The prophecy at his birth was that he would reign but die young, slain by the Aelf sword that his father the old Caan wore that day. So the old Caan gave the boy the sword, and the Black Tijanamir locked it away in a trunk in a sealed vault.

BLACK KNIGHT the third knight (after Leort and Woddet) to challenge Able at the pass (II, chap. 13, 152). His device is a skull. Beneath this disguise he is Duke Marder of Sheerwall, which is why Woddet tried to kill Able before the Black Knight came.

BLACKMANE Ravd's charger (I, chap. 4, 41).

BLOOD OF THE DRAGON Smiler's royal ancestor, whose spirit returns to engender heirs (II, chap. 38, 452). Grengarm is the dragon.

BLUE TI|ANAMIR the old Caan's fifth-born son, whose fate foretold that he would reign but drown young. Shortly after he became caan, "The dagger of a man-at-arms pierced his lungs, so that he drowned in his own blood" (II, chap. 37, 443).

BLUESTONE CASTLE Indign's castle on Bluestone Island, wrecked by Osterling pirates (I, chap. 2, 25).

BLUESTONE ISLAND a high, rocky island about a quarter of a mile from the mainland near Irringsmouth (I, chap. 2, 24).

BODACHAN Earth Aelf (I, chap. 3, 35). The Bodachan are one of the small clans. The "brown girl," a woman-deer Able sees twice (I, chap. 9, 73; I, chap. 10, 77), is probably one of the couple who give him Gylf (I, chap. 10, 79–81). Since the male is probably King Brunman himself, "brown girl" is probably his wife and queen of the clan.

BOLD BERTHOLD the peasant, originally from Griffinsford, who takes in Able, believing him to be his long lost brother, the real Able (I, chap. 2, 27; 29). He is the first-born child of Black Berthold and Mag. He fought against the raiding giants who destroyed his village. His brains were addled by a head wound and the torture of the giants. He was subsequently persecuted by Fire Aelf (I, chap. 38, 239). Bold Berthold seems 30 or 40 years older than Able (I, chap. 25, 162). He disappears at around the time when Disira is killed (I, chap. 10,

76). Able then assumes he is dead, but it turns out he is enslaved by Seaxneat's outlaws and sold to giants (II, chap. 13, 150). Met again in Jotunland where, although blinded, he has found Gerda (I, chap. 65, 401). He fights at the River Battle and receives a spear wound in his abdomen (II, chap. 40, 473). Able breaks his oath by healing him (474), then through the magic helm, Able sees him as Ben (476). Later he slays King Schildstarr (477).
Onomastics: (German) "bright ruler."

BORDA a giantess, the captain of Queen Idnn's bodyguard (II, chap. 27, 335). She liked the way that Able deflected questions of Duke Marder. Uri says she is the one who gave Able the gift of the magic helm (II, chap. 30, 365).

BORGALMIR the right head of a two-headed giant, friend of Schildstarr (II, chap. 21, 253).
Myth: (Norse) "Mountain Yeller" or "Bear Yeller," a frost giant, grandson of Ymir.

BOWSTRING SPIRITS the string that Parka gives Able is one she has spun of severed lives, "of lives cut short . . . Maybe only because a woman cut them with her teeth for me. She may have ended the lives by that act" (II, chap. 19, 225). These many lives color Able's dreams when he sleeps: As he puts it, "I was somebody, then somebody different, and then somebody new" (I, chap. 45, 279). Among them are:

- A woman in labor (I, chap. 41, 257).
- A drowning rescuer drowned (257).
- A blind man dying in the snow, likely a slave of the giants (I, chap. 62, 381).
- A boy who falls into the cook fire and dies (I, chap. 68, 417).
- A spirit whom he can hear while awake, one who says a few words and sobs (II, chap. 19, 228)

BRANNE OF BROADFORD the first knight whom Able bests at halberts. Branne had been the victor the year before (II, chap. 30, 369).

Onomastics: close to the Irish names Brann (raven) and Brianne (strong).

BREGA a peasant woman who lives in Glennidam (I, chap. 6, 52). She tells Ravd about Seaxneat. Egil had knocked her down before.
Onomastics: close to the Welsh female name Bregus (meaning "frail").
Myth: (Irish) a mythological site, also known as Bregia, that is a great central plain.

BRIDGE OF SWORDS "Modgud guards the Bridge of Swords. If it were destroyed, no ghost could visit us, and there are those who would destroy it" (II, chap. 24, 294). The bridge to Hel's common realm of Death, as opposed to the heaven for heroes in Skai for those chosen by the Valkyries. Able seems to have visited it, which in Norse mythology was a rare thing done only by Hermod.

BRIGHTHILLS Escan's fine-wine producing manor (II, chap. 31, 377).

BROWN TI|ANAMIR the old Caan's second born son. The prophecy at his birth was that he would become caan but die young, trodden into the mire. Shortly after he became caan, he was trampled to death by Celidon horses (II, chap. 37, 443).

BRUNMAN King of the Bodachan (II, chap. 33, 396).

BURNING MOUNTAIN another name for MOUNTAIN OF FIRE (II, chap. 37, 441).

BYMIR the first Angrborn seen by Able (I, chap. 10, 75), spotted near the Irring River, upstream from Glennidam (I, chap. 12, 87). Bymir bought Bold Berthold as a slave shortly after Disira was killed by Seaxneat (I, chap. 66, 405). Met again in the giant's barn (I, chap. 67, 409). Able kills him with a spit in the kitchen.
Myth: close to the Norse Brimir, another name for Ymir, the first giant.

CAAN the title of the Osterling king.
Onomastics: From the Latin form of Khan, Mongolian word for king.

CALENDAR see HISTORY.

CARADOC see NAMES ON THE WIND.

CASPAR the chief warder at Sheerwall Castle (I, chap. 42, 261). He is under Master Agr (first mentioned in I, chap. 41, 257). He had been branded on his forehead for some offense (I, chap. 41, 262).
Onomastics: a Persian name meaning "treasure," it is also traditionally the name of the magus who brings the gift of gold to the Christ child.

CELIDON a big country, longer than it is wide, on the west coast of the continent (I, chap. 2, 29). Irringsmouth, Forcetti, and Kingsdoom are all towns in Celidon. The flag of Celidon is sea-blue, with the royal Nykr embroidered in gold (II, chap. 32, 388).

Ice forms in the harbor at Forcetti, suggesting it is located to the north of N40° latitude. Mangoes grow near the Mountain of Fire, suggesting a latitude of N20°. Sandhill is in a desert south of the Mountain of Fire.

Uri says "males claim the throne first in this Celidon" (II, chap. 34, 409), providing a dizzying hint of multiple Celidons.
Arthuriana: one of the twelve legendary battlegrounds of King Arthur. It is associated with the Caledonian Forest in Scotland.

CHAUS one of Gaynor's titles: "Countess of Chaus." There is also a Lamwell of Chaus. The word means "jungle cat," so presumably the arms would show cats.

CHILDREN OF THE DRAGON the Lothurlings' name for themselves (II, chap. 38, 452). Grengarm is the dragon.

CLI a villager of Griffinsford whom Mag remembers as having joined Black Berthold in singing to the Overcyns during the bad times before Mag was taken from the village (II, chap. 22, 264).
Onomastics: (Greek) *cli-*, used in such names as Clio, Cliantha, Cliara. Probably from Kleos (glory), such as Kleio, muse of historical poetry.

CLOUD the mount Able rides after visiting Skai, a gift of the Valfather (II, chap. 3, 35). Her horn is sprouting (II, chap. 28, 346), so she is a juvenile flying unicorn. She leaves Able after he first breaks his oath by calling in a storm to help his smaller force break through the Osterling siege of Redhall (II, chap. 36, 432). She comes back to save him in his contest against Smiler (II, chap. 38, 455).

COHN, MS. Able's teacher in America, mentioned for her dog, Ming Toy (I, chap. 63, 392).

COLDCLIFF Beel's father's castle (I, chap. 48, 301), which now belongs to Beel's brother (I, chap. 54, 337). This is where Idnn's little pony was impregnated by a knight's charger. After they returned home to Kingsdoom, the pony died giving birth.

COLLE a baron of Celidon, freed by Able from the dungeon at Thortower (II, chap. 35, 412).
Onomastics: Gaelic name meaning "dwells at the woodland."

COLLINS Arthur's English teacher in America (I, chap. 24, 156).
Onomastics: an Irish/Gaelic name, Colin/Coilin/Collin, meaning "virile."

COSMOLOGY the universe of *The Wizard Knight* is made up of seven levels or worlds arranged in a stack, from highest to lowest:

1. Elysion—world of the Highest God.
2. Kleos—world of the angels.
3. Skai—world of the Overcyns, where twenty years of time are just a few days on Mythgarthr.
4. Mythgarthr—world of humankind, where time flows at the same rate as on Earth.
5. Aelfrice—world of the Aelf, where in one case six hours of time are a few days on Mythgarthr. But the ratios are not stable: at one point Disiri meets Able and assumes a year has passed for him, but it has only been a day; Toug's time in Aelfrice seems close to this ratio, since years go by in Mythgarthr for his few days in Aelfrice.
6. Muspel—world of dragons, including Grengarm and Setr.
7. Niflheim—world of the Lowest God.

Escan says that the worlds grow smaller from top to bottom.

Most levels have more than one world, as Able tells Toug, "The highest level, and the lowest, have only got one [world]. The rest have several. This is Dream. It's on the midmost level, with Mythgarthr"

(II, chap. 5, 53). It seems likely that Earth is also on the fourth level, and possibly Hel's realm of death as well.

Myth: Norse myth has "nine worlds" arranged on Yggsdragil, the giant ash tree of the universe. Midgard is in the middle, with Asgard above it, and Niflheim below it in the roots. The names and locations of the other six worlds are more sketchy: Muspell (with two Ls, the world of primordial fire and fire giants), Vanaheim, Jotunheim, Alfheim (home of the light elves), Svartalfaheim (home of the dark elves), and Hel.

COTH duke who was second to Arnthor until he was killed, two days before Able and his ragtag group arrived at the Mountain of Fire (II, chap. 37, 441).
Onomastics: Old Cornish word for "old." There is also a German word, *köth*, for a day laborer, a cottager who owned no farmland.

COUNT a noble rank between baron and duke, the only example in the text being the Countess of Chaus (one of Gaynor's titles).

CROL Beel's herald, who helps Able when he meets Beel's party (I, chap. 47, 292). His beard is black, but his face is so old that Able wonders if the beard is dyed (294). Crol has many cats (I, chap. 48, 297). Gilling kills him in a fit of pique (II, chap. 12, 138).
Onomastics: Middle Dutch word for "curly-headed." Also Polish *Krol*, an occupational name for someone who worked in a royal household.

DANDUN a baron of Celidon freed by Able from the dungeon of Thortower (II, chap. 35, 419).
Onomastics: perhaps Dan ("a Dane") plus the Dutch *dun* ("slender") for "slender Dane."

DAUNTE "Duchess of Daunte" is one of Gaynor's titles. English word for *enduring, obstinate.*

DEIF a villager of Griffinsford who was bitten by a two-headed turtle (II, chap. 22, 264).
Onomastics: Middle Scots word for "deaf."

DIRMAID see SPELL OF DIVINATION.

DISIRA Seaxneat's wife, mother of Ossar (I, chap. 6, 53). She is small, with black hair and very white skin (54). To Ravd her name is disturbingly close to Disiri. One wonders if she might be a priestess of the Moss Queen, particularly since Ulfa mentions that there are rites the villagers perform but cannot speak of (I, chap. 8, 62). Disiri, for her part, seems to set Able to protect Disira and Ossar. Later Seaxneat kills her while Able is out hunting (I, chap. 10, 76).

DISIRI the queen of the Moss Aelf (I, chap. 7, 57). She was worshipped in Glennidam: Able says to young Toug, "Some people in your village pray to Disiri. Your sister told me" (II, chap. 3, 35). Disira's name is a strong indication of this.

Piecing the puzzle together, it appears that before Griffinsford fell, Disiri took the real Able away, probably to the Isle of Glas to visit his mother. Then she switched Arthur Ormsby (of America) with the real Able. After Able delivers the message to Arnthor, he regains memories of childhood: playing with Disiri when both were young children (II, chap. 33, 404).

Myth: (Norse) Dísir are female supernatural beings; goddesses (Davidson).

DOLLOP AND SCALLOP the inn where Able and Pouk stay in Forcetti (I, chap. 33, 205). Owned by Gorn.

DON QUIXOTE (cross-reference from Quixote and Dunsany, Lord) a Spanish novel in two parts, first published in 1605 and 1615, and long considered a founding work of modern Western literature.

The hero is a middle-aged man who, having read too much chivalric romance, decides to live the life himself. In this form of literary-madness, he gives himself a title ("Don Quixote"), decides a farm girl is his lady love, declares his bony horse a magnificent charger, etc.

In the first book, his concerned friends try to cure him of his madness. In the second book, he returns to reality with a life-threatening melancholy, so that the concerned friends must try to engage his happy mania again. They cannot, and he dies, sane in mind but broken in spirit.

Commentary: because of the two-book nature of *Don Quixote*, and Able's possible madness, *The Wizard Knight* itself may be only a delusion of Arthur Ormsby, wounded or ill in an ambulance in America.

DRAKORITTER Able's name among the Overcyns (II, chap. 20, 235). Able's twenty-year career in Skai includes a number of details, not the least of which is that Overcyns often thought Ler was his brother. He visited the Bridge of Swords, which is something Hermod did in Norse myth. Able was at the siege of Nastrond. For a time he was on loan to the Lady. He was with Thunnor on the adventure where the place they had camped in turned out to be a giant's glove.
Onomastics: (Germanic) "dragon-rider," where "ritter" is a term signifying "knight."

DREAM another world on the fourth level, next to Mythgarthr (II, chap. 5, 53).

DUACH see NAMES ON THE WIND.

DUKE the upper nobility, second only to royalty, the ruler of a duchy. From Latin *dux,* a military commander. Dukes in the text include Bahart, Coth, Indign, Marder, and Thoas.

DUNS Uns's older brother (mentioned in I, chap. 35, 222; and met in I, chap. 38, 234). He is expected to inherit the farm. Org broke his arms when Duns tried to catch the ogre.
Onomastics: close to the English male name Dun, meaning "dark." Or a possible pun on "dunce." Also the word *duns* is the plural of *dun,* an Irish hill fort. (For a similar case, see LIS, LADY.)

DUNSANY, LORD the author to whom *The Wizard* is dedicated. Lord Dunsany (1878–1957) was an author of fantasy works. His poem "The Riders," quoted at the beginning of *The Knight,* was first published in *Fifty Poems* (1929) and collected in the Ballantine Adult Fantasy title *Beyond the Fields We Know.* "The Riders" mentions Quixote, for which see entry on DON QUIXOTE.

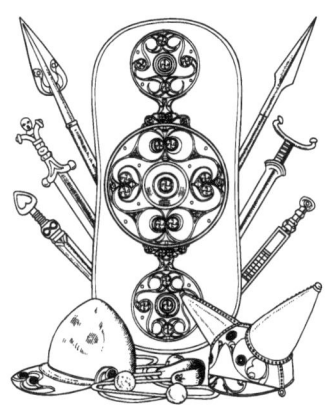

EARL MARSHAL see ESCAN.

EAST HALL Woddet's manor (I, chap. 34, 209).

EGIL one of the outlaws near Glennidam (I, chap. 6, 52), the one who knocked Brega down (53).
Myth: (Norse) "inspires fright." There are two characters with this name in Norse mythology. One is a brother of mighty smith Volund (also known as WELAND) and the husband of Valkyrie Olrun, said by some sources to be an excellent archer. The other is a character who took care of Thor's goats while he was on expedition to visit the giant HYMIR.

EGR one of Beel's upper servants, who is in charge of the baggage train (I, chap. 47, 293).
Onomastics: possibly the Russian name Egor, form of George ("farmer"); or the Old Norse Ægir, meaning "sea."

EILHART see NAMES ON THE WIND.

ELUNED, DAME the wife of Sir Owan, who asks the Earl Marshal for judgment (II, chap. 29, 352).
Onomastics: (Welsh) name, from *eilun*, meaning "image, idol."

ELYSION the world where the Most High God lives, above all the rest (II, chap. 7, 83). See COSMOLOGY.
Myth: (Greek) the name of a section of the Underworld reserved for the souls of the heroic and virtuous. Latinized as Elysium; the Elysian Fields.

ERAC one of Arnthor's own knights. He and Manasen escort Able to the dungeon below Thortower (II, chap. 33, 398).
Onomastics: close to the Irish name Erc, which means "red."
Arthuriana: a knight of the Round Table, also known as Errak(e), husband of Enid.

ESCAN the Earl Marshall, a nobleman of many titles (II, chap. 29, 351). He has an estate at Brighthills (II, chap. 31, 377). He has four manors and a castle (379); the castle is Sevengates (II, chap. 36, 425). He goes to Aelfrice with Able by way of the dungeons of Thortower (II, chap. 35, 419-24). Payn is his bastard (425).

In Aelfrice he says, "I wish I could sit here forever" (424), and even though he returns to Mythgarthr, he leaves a physical reflection behind in Aelfrice. This spirit twin seems alive, which makes it something like a changeling, doppleganger, or clone. In this regard, see MAG.
Arthuriana: Escan was the Duke or Earl of Cambenic in the early days of Arthur's reign. Along with a number of other kings, he revolted against Arthur, and suffered defeat at the battle of Bedegraine. Escan came back to Arthur's side to expel the Saxons.

ETELA a slave girl owned by the giant Logi, a smith in the town outside of Utgard (II, chap. 16, 185). Toug narrowly stops Org from kill-

ing her, and she tells Toug that the giants are making picks and shovels. Vil is her father or her stepfather, Lynnet her mother. According to Vil, Etela fears him because he is a conjurer and he told her if she was bad he would turn her into a doll (II, chap. 22, 271–72).
Onomastics: (Hebrew) Etel means "noble."

ETERNE the Mother of all Swords, the seventh brand Weland made. Eterne is haunted and commands the ghosts of those who bore it unworthily (I, chap. 9, 69). Hunbalt was one, and Skoll was the last to bear her before Grengarm captured her. When Able uses his final question to ask Michael what question he should ask, Michael says, "You should ask whence came the tongs that grasped Eterne. Notice, please, that I did not say I would answer you" (I, chap. 44, 277). See also ZIO.
Onomastics: [ih-TURN] archaic adjective meaning "eternal." Middle English, from Old French, from Latin *aeturnus*.

F

FARVAN Able's puppy in Aelfrice (II, chap. 40, 477). Its head is white with red ears.
Onomastics: (Scottish Gaelic) *farbhonn* (inner sole of a shoe) or *barbheann* (mountain with cliffs).
Myth: (Scotland) name of a fairy dog loosed upon Hugh MacLeod when he stole a treasured cup from the Realm of Fairy.
Commentary: the pup's coloration matches the pattern for Celto-British hell hounds (they are either all black or white with red ears).

FATHER Able, in trying to establish his social ranking in Celidon, says that his father sold hardware (I, chap. 47, 294). This finds a parallel with Black Berthold, who was probably a blacksmith.

FENRIR "as bad as the Giants of Winter and Old Night ever get. He bit off the arm of an Overcyn" (II, glossary) (II, chap. 3, 36).
Myth: (Norse) "fen dweller," mythic name for a monster wolf said to

be son of Loki by Angrboda. It was bound by Tyr, but it bit off his arm, and will break free at Ragnarok.

FIACH a warder in the dungeon under Thortower (II, chap. 33, 400). Able tries to make a deal with him, offering two years of gold rent upfront. Fiach wants to do it the old way. Able lets Org eat him. *Onomastics:* (Irish) a mythic name, derived from a word for "raven."

FINEFIELD Garvaon's manor, a big house with a wall around it and a tower (I, chap. 57, 356).

FIRE AELF the clan Setr took over completely (I, chap. 23, 144). The human smith Weland had been their king, but, as the armorer in Forcetti says, the Dragon got him. (Thus Setr must have killed Weland.) Baki and Uri are Fire Aelf. Bold Berthold was sometimes bothered by Fire Aelf, and Baki's behavior with the blind smith Vil is probably a good example of what this is like.

FIVE FATES the old Caan's wife, having been barren, suddenly gave birth to six boys. As each came forth, he was marked with a colored ribbon around his ankle: red, brown, white, gold, blue, and black. The fates of the six were foretold: Red to be crushed, Brown would be trod into mire, White to die at the hands of his followers, Golden would perish in a gold fortress, Blue to drown, and Black would be run through with the Aelf sword the old Caan wore the day the prophesy was made (II, chap. 37, 441–43). Five of the deaths happened at the Battle of Five Fates.
Commentary: the colors and their sequence seem relevant to the color symbolism of the Mongols and Central Asian people in general. Red is the color of the south; white is the color of the west; blue is the color of the east; black is the color of the north; and gold is the color of the center. For the Mongol Empire, their western-most territory was initially divided into White Horde and Blue Horde (west and east); when these were united through conquest, it became the

Golden Horde (center/combined). Historically there were White Khans, Blue Khans, and Golden Khans (but never Red Khans nor Black Khans).

The tijanamirs include brown, the only one that is not a direction color. While there is no center number in an even-numbered series, it is very interesting to see that Wolfe places the golden tijanamir between, or in the center of, white and blue.

FIVE REALMS the gold coins of Able's loot from Jotunland are of "five realms" (II, chap. 28, 347). Presumably these realms are:
1. Celidon.
2. Osterland.
3. Realm of the Dragon, land of Lothurlings.
4. Jotunland.
5. Unnamed southern realm, located south of the Greenflood.

FLINTWAL a giant stronghold owned by Thiaz (II, chap. 8, 88).

FOLKVANGER the Lady's house (II, chap. 3, 39).
Myth: (Norse) Folkvang ("field of the host") is the abode of the goddess Freyja.

FORCETTI Marder's town, a seaport near Sheerwall Castle (I, chap. 4, 42). Said to be named after an Overcyn (II, chap. 3, 36). It is located far enough to the north to guarantee that seasonal ice will form in the harbor (estimated to be around 40° north latitude).
Geography: Forcett is a village in north Yorkshire.
Onomastics: an Italian surname [for-CHEH-tee].
Myth: (Norse) Forseti, a law god, is son of Baldr and Nanna. His name means "chairman." At his father's hall, "Forseti/ spends all day long/ settling all suits-at-law" (*Prose Edda*, 55).

FOREST FIGHT a battle between the Osterlings and the Celidonian forces, told by Woddet (II, chap. 38, 457) and dreamed about by Able (459). Duke Marder and half-giant Heimer were there, so it was after the Battle of Utgard, and presumably while Able was in the dungeon at Thortower. It occurs after the Battle of Five Fates. "The Black Caan won it, in the end, but his camp had been sacked, and the war that seemed nearly over had become a long struggle" (II, chap. 39, 459). Following this setback, the Black Caan outflanks Arnthor and takes Kingsdoom and Thortower, sacking them both and butchering thousands.

FOX, THE a Lothurling god referred to by Stonebowl (II, chap. 39, 465). Probably Lothur himself, whom Able described as being "clever and cruel as a den of foxes" (II, chap. 37, 449).

FREE COMPANIES the polite name for outlaw gangs (I, chap. 4, 40).

FRIGG the Valfather's queen and Thunor's mother (II, chap. 3, 36). "She is a beautiful quiet lady everybody loves" (II, glossary).
Myth: (Norse) wife of Odin and Queen of Asgard, associated with fertility. She is not so clearly the mother of Thor, who is said to be Earth herself.

FROST GIANTS the Angrborn, especially the raiders (I, chap. 5, 47). They come in the cold weather because they cannot tolerate heat.

G

GALAAD a knight Able knew in Skai, along with Gamuret (II, chap. 13, 154).
Arthuriana: Galahad, the son of Lancelot and the perfect Grail knight.

GALENE a beggar woman Able found in ruinous Kingsdoom after it had fallen to the Osterlings (II, chap. 36, 429).
Myth: (Greek) a sea nymph or goddess, her name means "calm seas."

GAMURET a knight Able knew in Skai, along with Galaad (II, chap. 13, 154).
Arthuriana: Parsifal's father.

GARSECG a name used by Setr when he meets Able (I, chap. 22, 137). It is his water name. (First mentioned in I, chap. 1, 21.) An early aside that he taught Able strength and speed (I, chap. 13, 93). As the old Sea Aelf he is similar to Proteus of Greek myth.

Onomastics: (Old English) poetic term for "ocean." Davidson says it literally means "spear-man."

GARVAON Beel's best knight. He teaches Able how to fight with a sword (I, chap. 55, 340-43; Garvaon is also mentioned in I, chap. 13, 93 and I, chap. 47, 293). He is 38 years old (I, chap. 57, 355), 22 years older than Idnn, who is 16. Finefield is his manor (I, chap. 49, 306). His emblem is a tree. His wife died two years before he met Able (355). He loves Idnn and hopes to win her, asking Able not to be his rival, but he doesn't realize her fate until rather late.

Just before the battle against Setr, Able seems to say that Garvaon killed Gilling: "What you did I judge to be no crime. Neither the first time nor the second time" (II, chap. 26, 324). More specifically, Able says that just before the discovery of Gilling's body, Garvaon's men had been frightened by something they had just seen a moment before (II, chap. 20, 244), i.e., they had seen Garvaon strike Gilling the second time.

Garvaon is part of the group that kills Setr, and with his dying breath he seems to confess to Able that he killed Gilling: "You knew. Tell her I loved her" (326). It seems odd since he was fighting against giants at the time of Gilling's first stabbing (II, chap. 12, 140-41), but in addition to other mundane angles, there is also the paradoxical possibility that Garvaon revisted the scene from Skai, just as Able as a green knight visited himself drinking water at Bluestone Island.
Onomastics: The Old English *gar* means spear and *wine* means friend, so Garvaon might be "spear-friend," a variant of Garvin ("friend in battle").

GAWAIN "I did not speak; but in my mind Gawain knelt again, baring his neck" (II, chap. 26, 316). Able's role as a "green knight" seems to have extended to his being the Green Knight, or re-enacting the role in Skai. See GREEN KNIGHT.
Arthuriana: the hero of *Sir Gawain and the Green Knight* (ca. A.D. 1400).

GAYNOR Arnthor's wife, the Queen of Celidon (mentioned in I, chap. 19, 123; met in II, chap. 31, 377). Her titles include Countess of Chaus and Duchess of Daunte (II, chap. 33, 394). She is nearly the same age as Idnn, who is 16; they were friends at court and grew up together (II, chap. 31, 377).
Arthuriana: Guenevere, wife of King Arthur and mistress of Lancelot du Lac. Forms of her name include Guinevere, Gwenhwyfar (Welsh), Guenhumare, Ginevra, and Gaynour (Middle English).

GED a warder in the dungeon under Thortower (II, chap. 35, 411).
Onomastics: the pet form of the English name Gerard, "spear strong."

GERDA the girl Bold Berthold was going to marry, she was taken by giants in a raid (met in I, chap. 64, 395; named in I, chap. 65, 401). When she meets Able she can see "the old lady" with him, presumably the witch-ghost Huld. She has two teenage-seeming children, half-giants Heimir and Hela, by the giant Hymir. She is owned by Hymir's son Hyndle when Able meets her. Her name and position echo that of Geri (Ben's girlfriend in America), yet through the magic helm, while Able sees that Bold Berthold looks like Ben, Gerda does not look like Geri; she looks like a younger Gerda.
Myth: (Norse) Gerda (Gerdr, Gerth, or Gerthr), daughter of the frost giant Gymir and Angurboda, was so beautiful she attracted the god Frey. He despaired of winning her since the giants were his enemies. His clever servant won her for him. Her union with Frey is seen as the surrender of frost to spring.

GERI the girl Ben was dating when Able lost America (I, chap. 1, 19).
Myth: (Norse) one of two wolves, Freki and Geri, to whom Odin gives his food when he sits and feasts with the warriors of the Einherjar in Valhall.

GEROR a god or goddess of the giants (II, chap. 15, 169).
Myth: (Norse) alternate spelling of Gerd, an Old Norse name meaning "guarded, protected." Also known as GERDA, which see.

GERRUNE the fifth knight Able faced at halberts (II, chap. 30, 369). A big man, a free lance. Though Able bests him, Gerrune is declared the victor. When the honor battle between Queen Gaynor and Princess Morcaine comes up, many suppose he will be the queen's champion (II, chap. 32, 387). He is one of the five who stay through the end of Able's fight against Loth (II, chap. 32, 391).

GIANTS giant blood is full of creatures: "I was tempted to stamp on the ugly little creatures that swam in it" (I, chap. 67, 411).

GIF a slave of Logi (II, chap. 17, 195). Probably one of the two women sleeping on the hearth (191). Later one of the two women being sorted out (II, chap. 21, 251), she becomes one of Svon's slaves (II, chap. 23, 277). She had been paired to Rowd in Logi's house.
Onomastics: possibly from *gif gaff,* used by Sir Walter Scott as meaning "good turn for good turn." Possibly related to Old Norse *gefa* (to give) and *gjof* (gift).

GILLING the King of the Angrborn (II, chap. 6, 68). Upon taking the throne he put down a rebellion (II, chap. 8, 88). Gilling wants the green knight. To get him, he obtains the knight's cat (Mani) and asks him the knight's name. Toug tells them it is Sir Able (89). See MYSTERY OF KING GILLING'S MURDER.
Myth: (Norse) "screamer," a giant who is the father of Suttung. He is drowned by two dwarfs who had previously slain Kvasir.

GLENNIDAM the village where Ulfa and Toug were born (I, chap. 4, 38). It is located on a stream that must be named the Glenny, and they presumably have a dam on it. The population is around 53. Baki tells Toug the village revered the Aelf because Disiri was kind, offering to hide their children when the Angrborn came (II, chap. 17, 191). This sounds a lot like what happened with the real Able in the next village of Griffinsford. A mix of villagers and outlaws includes: Brega, Disira, Egil, Haf, Hulta, Old Toug, Ossar, Seaxneat, Toug, Ulfa, Ulfa's mother, Vali, and Ve.

GLUMMNIR a champion among the giants, a peer of Schildstarr (II, chap. 12, 135).
Onomastics: Glúmr, originally a nickname related to Modern Norwegian *glum,* "a person with a glowering expression."

GOLDEN TI|ANAMIR the old Caan's fourth son. According to prophesy, he would reign but die young in a golden fortress. His helmet was gold in color, just as those of his brothers bore their name colors. Shortly after he became caan, he led his elephants against Woddet. "Sir Woddet's point entered the eye socket, and the Golden Caan died in that fortress of gold" (II, chap. 37, 443).

GOLDENLAWN the manor Lynnet came from (II, chap. 22, 259). Located just a few miles north of Redhall, it has a garden grotto built by her father for her mother. This grotto is practically a shrine to Disiri and she seems to use it as such with Able (II, chap. 27, 339).

GORN the innkeeper at the Dollop and Scallop (I, chap. 36, 228; first met 223). He tries to overcharge Able. Then he sets Sir Nytir on him.
Onomastics: Old Norse word for guts/bowels.

GOTTFRIED see NAMES ON THE WIND.

GRANDMOTHER when Ulfa tries to seduce Able, "she was rubbing herself against me, reminding me of grandma's cat" (I, chap. 8, 63). This is one of the few traces of Able's grandmother. One of the puzzles about his American past is how he managed to be raised by his brother Ben when both boys were orphaned at a young age. The solution would seem to be that their grandmother moved into their house and cared for them. Even though they had an adult guardian, Ben still raised Able in the sense of teaching him the Male Mysteries.

Other than this, we know that Able's grandparents were farmers.

GREEN KNIGHT Able, with his blank green shield, is referred to as the green knight. But the famous Green Knight is another sort of wizard knight from the days of King Arthur who allows his head to be cut off by Sir Gawain in exchange for the opportunity to give Gawain a similar blow in one year.

GREENFLOOD a river south of Burning Mountain (II, chap. 38, 455), presumably the border between Celidon and the southern realm. The Lotherling overseas expeditionary force led by Smiler seems to have made landfall south of the river.

GRENGARM the dragon who has Eterne and has taken over the grotto of the Griffin (I, chap. 68, 422; mentioned in I, chap. 9, 69). Grengarm is also the dragon spirit who impregnates the Lothurling Queen, as the name list makes plain in the entry for Smiler: "This is what we called the Dragon Prince. The dragon was Grengarm" (II, glossary).

A group of Aelf (including Uri) placed a female sacrifice for him at the altar of the Griffin (I, chap. 68, 422). She turns out to be Morcaine. Able kills Grengarm and his picture adorns Able's shield.
Myth: (Norse) perhaps a blend of Grendal and Garm. Grendal is the monster of the fen in the poem *Beowulf*. Garm is the underworld dog who kills Tyr at Ragnarok.

GRIFFIN the little river running past Griffinsford and into the Irring (I, chap. 2, 26). The source of the Griffin is within a cave in the mountains bordering Jotunland (I, chap 68, 419). The outside of the cave seems to be carved like a griffin, but it is really a petrified griffin. Inside the grotto the dragon Grengarm guards a hoard of treasure, including the sword Eterne.

GRIFFINSFORD a village the Angrborn raiders wiped out, located at a crossing point on the Griffin (I, chap. 1, 20). Its inhabitants included Baldig, Black Berthold, Bold Berthold, Cli, Deif, Gerda, Grumma, Mag, the real Able, Skjena, Uld, and Wer.

GROA one of the women on the Isle of Glas (II, chap. 22, 263). She carved an image of the Lady for them, "but another came by night and broke it, leaving an image of herself by the pool, beautiful beyond woman." Groa taught Mag how to write.
Myth: (Norse) a sibyl who was wife to Aurvandil the Brave. She worked to heal Thor's head-wound but he distracted her, so the hone (a fine-grained whetstone for sharpening tools) is still stuck in his head.

GRUMMA a villager of Griffinsford who was bitten by a two-headed turtle (II, chap. 22, 264).
Onomastics: perhaps a female version of (Scandinavian) Grummi, meaning "cruel one."

GYLF Able's dog (I, chap. 11, 80). The Valfather lost him and Able gets to keep him until the Valfather wants him back. Able gets him from two Bodachan (a brown woman/deer and a man), who take baby Ossar in exchange. Frightened of how the dog changes into a large monster when in combat, Able abandons him before Irringsmouth, but Gylf follows and hides on the ship *Western Trader*. After Able is badly wounded, he sends Gylf to find help from Aelfs. Garsecg chains Gylf in a cave (I, chap. 63, 392–93) before going to aid Able (I, chap. 39, 242), but eventually Gylf breaks free (243). Gylf catches up with Able at Forcetti, snatching food at the inn Dollop and Scallop and finally coming when Able calls outside the farmhouse (240).
Myth: (Norse) Gylfi, an early king of Sweden who let Gefion take Zealand. He appears in the *Prose Edda* as the questioner of the Gods. See OSSAR; FARVAN.

H

HAF one of the two boys who tries to rob Able on the road between Irringsmouth and Griffinsford (I, chap. 2, 27; II, chap. 1, 20). Young Toug is the other one, and Able at that time is younger still.
Onomastics: Old Icelandic word for "sea."

HALWEARD the steward Marder sent to Redhall (II, chap. 27, 338).
Onomastics: Anglo-Scandinavian form of Hallvardr (Halvard), literally "rock guardian" (stolid defender).

HE WHO SMILES the formal name of Smiler, the Lothurling leader (II, chap. 38, 452). A Chinese proverb says, "He who smiles in a crisis has found someone to blame." A Japanese proverb goes, "He who smiles rather than rages is always the stronger."

HEIMIR Gerda's half-giant son by Hymir, he tries to sneak up on Able's camp at night, but then he runs off (II, chap. 7, 75; he is first

mentioned in I, chap. 28, 175). He and his younger sister Hela are welcomed into Able's group. He is a head taller than Hela (I, chap. 10, 76), so he must be around 8' 8". He was turned out of the house when he reached a certain age, as happens with half-giant males.
Myth: (Norse) foster-father of Valkyrie Brynhild.

HEL the Overcyn woman in charge of death (I, chap. 69, 424). Her realm is across the Bridge of Swords, presumably located on the fourth level (along with Dream and Earth).

Obviously warriors hope to earn a place elsewhere: Arnthor fears that he will not be worthy of the Valkyries (II, chap. 39, 466) but he hopes he might be included among the phantom heroes of the sword Eterne (467), rather than being relegated to the drab place of common death. But there is a worse place than that, as revealed when Ravd says to Brega, "If you break that oath, Hel will condemn your spirit to Muspel, the Circle of Fire" (I, chap. 6, 52).
Myth: (Norse) daughter of Loki, she is Queen of the Dead.

HELA Gerda's half-giant daughter by Hymir (II, chap. 7, 79). "She said she was dumb because she was too smart to say she was smart" (II, glossary). She falls in love with the Knight of the Sun, Sir Woddet. She is eight feet tall (I, chap. 10, 76). She is Heimir's little sister (I, chap. 64, 398), and she voluntarily followed him into exile.
Myth: (Norse) another name for Hel.

HEREWOR herald of Sir Woddet (II, chap. 13, 154).
Onomastics: probably related to Old English Hereweald, like Harald, i.e., herald.

HERMAD one of Marder's knights, he attacks Able on the practice field and gets all his ribs broken (I, chap. 33, 204).
Myth: seems close to Norse Hermod, son of Odin, who rode to Hel to seek Balder.

HERN THE HUNTER a name sometimes used for the Valfather when he hunts giants in animal form with a pack of dogs like Gylf (II, chap. 5, 54).
Myth: (English) a mythic hunter.

HISTORY two timelines for *The Wizard Knight*.

TIMELINE 2002

Assuming that Able leaves America in 2001 and arrives in Irringsmouth in the minimal amount of time, in 2002; and that Mag is a clone of the girl who will become Mrs. Ormsby in America (where the real girl emerged in an America decades after she left).

-1000 years	War between Aelf and Setr (I, chap. 26, 165), circa A.D. 1000 (according to Setr, but he is a liar).
-58 years?	Bold Berthold born (A.D. 1943).
-55 years?	The real Able born, then Mag disappears, taken by dragon Setr to Glas.
-50 years?	Black Berthold dies; Bold Berthold raises his little brother, the real Able (A.D. 1951).
-39 years?	The real Able leaves Mythgarthr, stays in Aelfrice for many Aelf years; Bold Berthold fights giants and is wounded; Gerda captured, enslaved. Griffinsford destroyed (A.D. 1962).
-30 years	The tradition of knights at the ford ends.
-22 years	Arnthor becomes king of Celidon (A.D. 1979).
-19 years	Ben is born in America (A.D. 1982).
-16 years	Arthur is born; Mrs. Ormsby vanishes (A.D. 1985).
-11 years?	Mr. Ormsby dies in America. Ben (8) raises his little brother (5) with his grandmother.
-10 years	Idnn is born in Celidon; Lynnet is captured by raiding giants, enslaved.

-1 year	FALL 2001. Arthur walks from the cabin to Mythgarthr, then is pulled into Aelfrice.
1 year	SPRING 2002. Able arrives in Mythgarthr. Missing time of one season, perhaps 100 days, presumably the period when Disiri and the Aelf kings were loading the message into his mind in Aelfrice. He meets Bold Berthold, who takes him for the real Able.
	SUMMER. Able meets Sir Ravd. Leads Ravd and Svon to Glennidam. While searching for Disira he meets Disiri and she makes him a man (aging him less than ten years). He returns, takes young Toug on trip to Aelfrice, rescues Disira and takes her to Berthold's hut where they dawdle for weeks until summer is over.
	FALL. Seaxneat kills Disira, and Bold Berthold is missing, presumed dead, so Able goes out to clean up the outlaw forest. Later he goes to sea, is wounded, and goes to Aelfrice where three years pass on Mythgarthr.
4 years	Garvaon's wife dies in childbirth (I, chap. 57, 355); in late fall Able returns to Mythgarthr from Aelfrice, goes to Mountain of Fire, takes a short trip to Muspel that adds one year in Mythgarthr time.
5 years	Able, Pouk, and Thunrolf in down levels.
6 years	SPRING. At Forcetti Able gets quest to hold pass.
	SUMMER. He ditches squire Svon in late June or early July (I, chap. 44, 272). He asks to borrow a horse from Beel (I, chap. 48, 297). Late Summer when Able goes after raiders (I, chap. 62, 379). Able kills Grengarm and dies. Able spends 20 years in Skai, comes back. After breaking through the giant ambush, Able takes a trip to Aelfrice with Gylf and Baki (314). Able fights Kulili, yields, and is spared (324). Able gets Garvaon, Svon, and Toug to fight Setr; Vil jumps on the dragon's back and chokes Setr using the magic bowstring he had stolen from Able (326).

SEPTEMBER. Garvaon is buried the day before the battle of the pass. After the battle, Queen Idnn says Able came to borrow a horse two months ago (II, chap. 27, 331).

FALL. Raid on Khazneh.

7 years   JANUARY. At Redhall, Halweard says it is winter, and after a brief meeting with Disiri, Able returns to Redhall with snow in his hair (II, chap. 27, 339). Able gives part of message to King Arnthor, is sent to dungeon.

FEBRUARY. Queen Idnn arrives at Kingsdoom; Able breaks parole; Battle of Five Fates.

MARCH. Able and Escan go to lower levels; Forest Fight.

JULY. From Aelfrice and below, Able and Escan return to find Kingsdoom in ruins and high summer (four months have passed in their absence). They go to Redhall, to Irringsmouth (hoping for a ship), down the coast to Forcetti, and then to Kingsdoom.

AUGUST. Three weeks from Kingsdoom to Mountain of Fire (II, chap. 37, 439).

SEPTEMBER. The River Battle.

TIMELINE 2041

Assuming that Able leaves America in 2001 and arrives in Irringsmouth in 2041; and Mrs. Ormsby is a serial mom who becomes Mag.

1982	Ben is born.
1985	Art is born, Mrs. Ormsby disappears/dies (post partum).
1986	Bold Berthold is born.
1989	The real Able is born; Mag disappears.
1990	Mr. Ormsby dies. Ben 8, Art 5.
2001	The real Able (age 12) goes to Aelfrice; Bold Berthold

	(age 15) fights against giants; Art (age 16) walks to Mythgarthr, ends up in Aelfrice for many Aelfrice years.
2030	Idnn born; Gaynor born (circa).
2041	Able (age 16/23) arrives in Mythgarthr in spring. Ben (59). Bold Berthold (55), who was once 1 year younger than Art, is now 32 years older.
2042	Able in Aelfrice.
2043	Able in Aelfrice.
2044	Able returns to Mythgarthr in late fall, then goes down levels.
2045	Able, Pouk, and Thunrolf in down levels.
2046	Able, Pouk, and Thunrolf return 1 year and 1 day.
2047	Able's visit to Redhall in winter marks beginning of seventh year.

HOB one of Caspar's warders (I, chap. 42, 263). He laughs at Able in a menacing way so Able beats him (261). This causes a problem, the solution being Able's temporary banishment (264). Later Hob is killed and eaten by Org (I, chap. 43, 267). This causes another problem, so Able has to take Org with him on his temporary banishment.
Myth: (British/Scottish) a figure of folklore, sometimes a kindly brownie, other times more dangerous. For example, Hob Headless, who haunted a road near the River Kent. "Confined under a rock for 99 years, Hob Headless trapped passersby who rested upon his rock, gluing them down so that they could not rise and escape" (Monaghan).

HORDSVIN the cook on the *Western Trader* (I, chap. 19, 125). He brings food down to a badly wounded Able in the cable tier. He says he and his helper Surt fought next to Able against the Osterling pirates.
Onomastics: possibly meaning "strong young man," from the Norse *hordr* (hard, strong) and *sveinn* (young man).

HROLFR a forester who used to work for Escan's father (II, chap. 36, 431). His wife was Amabel. They adopted Payn, Escan's bastard.
Onomastics: Norse name Hrolf means "wolf"; Hrolfr Kraki was a famous warrior king of Denmark.

HULD the witch who owned Mani (II, chap. 1, 21). Mani says she has been hovering around them ever since they left her house, hoping to do them a favor (II, chap. 4, 41), but she is not around anymore (presumably since she did a favor by appearing beside Able for Gerda [I, chap. 66, 406]). She also has information she gives to Able by way of Mani. She moans at the sight of Gerda's chains (II, chap. 7, 76). She tells Mani about Baki's injury (II, chap. 8, 85). She takes the shape of Idnn to tend Gilling while the real Idnn goes to find Able (II, chap. 14, 157).
Myth: (Norse) a witch who appears in the Ynglinsaga and the Starlingasaga. Her name derives from *hulda* (hiding, secrecy).

HULTA a woman in Glennidam, wife of Vali, mother of Ve (I, chap. 8, 65).
Onomastics: the similar name Hulda means "beloved" (German), "weasel" (Hebrew), "hidden" (Norse/Swedish).

HUNBALT a knight of Eterne (II, chap. 26, 320).
Onomastics: close to Hunbaut, eponymous hero of an early 13th century French romance.

HYMIR the Angrborn who got Gerda (first mentioned in I, chap. 64, 396). Father of giant Hyndle, and half-giants Heimir and Hela.
Myth: (Norse) sea giant with whom Thor went fishing on his expedition to catch the World Serpent.

HYNDLE "Hymir's Angrborn son" (I, glossary), Gerda's master, a giant (I, chap. 64, 396).
Myth: (Norse) seems close to Hyndla, a giantess who appears as the rival of Freyja.

I

IDNN Beel's daughter (first mentioned in I, chap. 19, 123). She is named after the goddess (II, chap. 12, 134). She is around sixteen years old. Afraid of her fate, she tries to talk Able into "rescuing" her, but he refuses. She cannot see that Garvaon loves her, and she fixes her sights on Svon. She becomes Queen of Jotunland when she marries King Gilling (II, chap. 13, 155). After he dies she marries Svon.

IDNN the goddess. Beel says of his daughter, "Her honesty rivals that of her patroness, and her wisdom the Lady's," to which a giant says of Overcyn Idnn, "Neither that false slut nor the witch her sister find favor among the sons of Angr, Southling" (II, chap. 12, 134). Thus she is said to be sister to the Lady.
Myth: (Norse) Idunn ("active in love") is the wife of Bragi (god of poetry) and the goddess who guards the golden apples of youth for the gods. I am unable to find a mention of her having a sister.

INDIGN the duke of northernmost Celidon, who owned Bluestone Castle (I, chap. 2, 25). The Osterling pirates killed him and razed the castle. His badge is the blue boar (26).

At first he is the most likely candidate for the phantom knight that Able sees upon drinking the water at Bluestone Island. Presumably the ghost would be a sign that Able should avenge his death and perhaps even take his place as local castle lord.

Onomastics: while there is a hint of *indigo*, a shade of blue, in his name, *indign* [in-DINE] is an obscure word meaning "unbecoming; undignified; disgraceful" (*Mrs. Byrne's*).

IRONMOUTH one of Smiler's knights, a Dragon Warrior (II, chap. 38, 452).

IRRING a big river in Celidon (I, chap. 10, 75).
Onomastics: perhaps from the German *irren* (to wander).

IRRINGSMOUTH Indign's town, a northern port where the Irring empties into the sea (I, chap. 2, 26). The Osterlings had burned a lot of it.

ISLE OF GLAS not really an island; rather, the top of the tower Setr built in Aelfrice (I, chap. 22, 140). There are trees and grass on it, and a pool that leads to Aelfrice. The durian fruit found growing here suggests that the island is located close to the equator.

Able climbs up the first time from Aelfrice. Later Vil, Toug, Etela, and Lynnet walk there by accident in the weird fog in Jotunland, but Able sees "another" with them, probably Mag (II, chap. 26, 316).

A generation earlier it has been a Siren Shoal, a private feeding area of Garsecg, stocked with beautiful women he had kidnapped, but when Able visits, it is long deserted. Later a bitter Able tells the Kingsdoom pages about Glas—that the women died, killed by one another or the seamen they tricked, until the last one took poison (II, chap. 35, 418).

JER the leader of the outlaw gang near Glennidam (I, chap. 12, 86).
Onomastics: (German) nickname of Jerry, "mighty spearman."

JOTUNHOME the secret country of the Angrborn women (II, chap. 16, 181). The land of the giantesses.
Myth: (Norse) Jotunheim, realm of the giants.

JOTUNLAND the Angrborn country, north of the Mountains of Mice (I, chap. 13, 93). The land of the giants.

K

KEI one of Arnthor's knights (II, chap. 31, 372). A fine jouster, he was champion of the year before. Able bests him, but they break six lances before Kei's mount goes down. Later he is chosen as the third champion in the three fights against Smiler's Dragon Warriors. He is killed by Ironmouth (II, chap. 38, 454).
Arthuriana: Kei (Caei, Keu, Kay, Cayous) is Arthur's seneschal (a type of high-powered bailiff, steward, or majordomo). He is a ubiquitous character in Arthurian romance but never a major one.

KELPIES Sea Aelf girls (I, chap. 21, 136).

KERL the first mate on the *Western Trader* (I, chap. 16, 109). He becomes captain after Able disappears into the sea and is still captain three years later when Able reappears (I, chap. 28, 174).
Onomastics: close to the Greek Keril meaning "lordly"; close to *churl*, "freeman, one without rank."

KHAZNEH a city of the Osterlings, located in or just beyond the Mountains of the Sun (II, chap. 11, 126). Woddet takes part in looting it in a raid that comes before the Battle of Five Fates.
Onomastics: (Arabic) "The Treasury," one of the most elaborate temple tombs in the ancient city of Petra, located in a rugged canyon of Jordan. As with most of the other buildings in this town, it is carved out of a sandstone rock face.

KHIMAIRAE Fire Aelf transformed into human-sized, winged dragons (I, chap. 23, 143), they are guardians of Glas, both the tower and the isle (I, chap. 22, 140).
Myth: (Greek) chimaerae, plural of chimaera, a shape-shifting, fire-breathing monster, often depicted as having the body of a lioness, with a tail ending in a serpent head, and the head of a goat coming out of its spine, in addition to the head of a lion.

KINGSDOOM a seaport, the capital of Celidon (I, chap. 31, 196). Thortower, Arnthor's castle, is located in the middle of the city (II, chap. 28, 348).

KIRSTEN a beloved servant who died when Lynnet was fourteen years old (II, chap. 22, 260).
Onomastics: Dutch/Norwegian form of Christiana. In Celidon, this might have a pre-Christian meaning of "anointed one."

KLEOS the second world, above Skai, where Michael lives (I, chap. 44, 275). Parka is said to come from Kleos, and Lothur might have, too. See COSMOLOGY.

Able writes, "I said [to Escan] that someday I would like to go to Kleos, the world above Skai; but it would be years before I tried" (II, chap. 35, 424).

KNIGHT OF THE SUN the second knight to fight Able at the mountain pass (II, chap. 11, 120). He is Woddet in disguise.

KNIGHTS Agr?, Arn?, Branne of Broadford, Erac, Galaad, Gamuret, Garvaon, Gawain, Gerrune, Hermad, Hunbalt, Kei, Lamwell of Chaus, Leort, Llwch, Lud, Manasen, Marc, Nopel, Nytir of Fairhall, Oriel Owan, Ravd of Redhall, Rober of Greenglory, Sabel, Skoll, Svon, Swit, Toug, Vidare, Woddet.

KNIGHTS OF ETERNE the phantom knights include Hunbalt and Skoll. At times there are eight; at other times there are more.

KULILI the person responsible for the Aelf (I, glossary). She knit herself out of worms, meaning she could unravel and scatter, making her hard to catch. Kulili is a composite of many individuals, or as Able puts it, "Kulili's the group mind of creatures who are largely unaware of their individual existences" (II, chap. 4, 46).

The Sea Aelf hope Able will fight her for them (I, chap. 21, 134). Kulili says the world known as Aelfrice was hers before there were any Aelf. She created Aelf to protect her forest. But they chased her from the land into the water, then from the water into the depths (I, chap. 27, 171).

Kulili looks like the statue "more beautiful than woman" Able sees on the Isle of Glas (I, chap. 27, 171). The White Dragon, first seen (II, chap. 26, 315), is identified as Kulili later in the same chapter (324). Able tells Arnthor, "The Most High God placed a numerous folk called Kulili. As we reverence the Overcyns, so Kulili was to reverence us, and did, and was revered by the dragons of Muspel" (II, chap. 33, 397). So it would seem that the dragon-form is revered by the dragons, and the woman-form is the reflection of her reverence for humans.

Myth: (Sumerian) a type of dragon, later a merman. Kulili portrayed as a dragon symbolizes chaos, but as a fishman, he symbolizes the forerunner of the Abgal (a group of water creatures).

KYOT see NAMES ON THE WIND.

L

LADY, THE a woman of the Overcyn, the Valfather's youngest daughter (I, chap. 2, 26), his most important daughter (I, chap. 21, 133). "No one is supposed to use her name in ordinary talk, so they say 'the Lady' instead" (I, glossary). The crescent moon is her bow (I, chap. 21, 132). Her perfume is lilac (II, chap. 10, 110). In Skai, Able was on loan to her for a time. Able tells Mani about her cats.
Myth: (Norse) Freyja (meaning "Lady"). She was born of the Vanir gods rather than the Æsir, daughter of Njord and possibly Nerthus. A goddess of love and death, she receives half of the knights the Valkyrie bring to Asgard. She is represented as riding in a chariot drawn by two cats.

LAEMPHALT the name Toug gave to the white stallion Beel had given to Able (II, chap. 3, 36).
Onomastics: perhaps Latin "white neck" (*laem* = throat, gullet; *phal* = shining, white).

LAMIAE plural of lamia.
Myth: (Greek) vampiric half-woman, half-serpent monster who devours children.

LAMWELL OF CHAUS a queen's house knight who is the second to lose to Able at halberts (II, chap. 30, 369). He is one of the five bravest knights at Thortower (II, chap. 32, 391). He comes to Redhall with news from King Arnthor in the south, in need of every man (II, chap. 36, 435). See also CHAUS.
Arthuriana: Sir Lamwell is a 16th century lay (song form of Northern Europe) surviving in three fragments, thought to be derived from a Middle English translation of Marie de France's *Lanval*. Lamwell is the hero of an "otherworld" adventure: he leaves Arthur's court after being treated unjustly and finds love with a fairy lady who swears him to secrecy.

LEESHA Lynnet's sister who died in childbirth (II, chap. 22, 260).
Onomastics: (Latin) "joy," from Lecia, short form of Leticia. Or perhaps a child's form of the Old German name Alicia, "noble, exalted."
Commentary: the names in this family all start with L: their mother is Lis; their father is Leifer. In Arthuriana, the sister of Lynette is Lyones.

LEIFR, LORD Lynnet's father, slain by the Frost Giants who stormed Goldenlawn (II, chap. 22, 260). She sees him in the Room of Lost Love.
Onomastics: (Old Norse) "descendant, heir."

LEORT the Knight of the Leopards (II, chap. 9, 96). He is the first knight to challenge Able at the pass. Travelling with him are a herald, a squire, two pages, men at arms, and seven manservants. His father owns Sandhill Castle. Mani notes his shield is "tastefully ornamented with spotted cats" (II, chap. 19, 218), and his pennon has seven leopards (II, chap. 11, 120). He is 24 years old but had been knighted at 19, which was considered early (II, chap. 9, 101).

Onomastics: it certainly looks like *leo* (lion), just like *leopard* (a portmanteau word combining *leo* the lion with *pard* the panther, to describe an animal thought by the ancients to be a hybrid). On the other hand, one source links it to Albert, a German name meaning "all bright/famous."

LER an Overcyn (II, chap. 7, 76). Able calls him "the sort of friend you do not have to talk to, and some people thought we were brothers" (II, glossary).
Myth: (Celtic) the Irish form of "sea," a god known as Lir, Llyr, and Lear.

LIS, LADY Lynnet's mother, Etela's grandmother (II, chap. 22, 260). Met in Room of Lost Love (II, chap. 22, 260), later met in the flesh (II, chap. 27, 337).
Onomastics: (Irish) "lis" is a word for a hill fort (along with rath, dun, and cashel); in this regard, see DUNS.

LLWCH a powerful knight of the Valfather who unseated Able at a joust in Skai (II, chap. 9, 96). "They said his sword leaped like fire, and it was true" (II, glossary).
Arthuriana: a legendary Welsh figure who bore a flaming sword as he led King Arthur through the dim otherworld.

LOGI the giant smith who owns many human slaves, including Alca, Etela, Gif, Lynnet, Rowd, Sceef, and Vil (II, chap. 16, 186). Met chasing Toug (II, chap. 17, 192). He grabs Toug, then Org grapples with Logi. Toug helps kill him.
Myth: (Norse) "flame," the giant competitor who beat Loki in an eating contest.

LOTH the dead knight Morcaine reanimated to be her champion. In life, his manor was Northolding, and his shield showed a black elk on a white field (II, chap. 32, 389). Able gave his sword to Wistan.
Onomastics: a surname of unknown meaning; English word for "un-

willingness," "reluctance," or "strongly opposed." In this sense, see INDIGN.

LOTHUR the Valfather's youngest son (II, glossary), or he was of a group that left Kleos (II, chap. 4, 48). Lothur fathered children upon Angr, the Angrborn (48; met in II, chap. 37, 446). Able calls him great prince of light, prince of fire (447).
Myth: (Norse) Lothur is another name for Odin's brother Ve, who is sometimes conflated with Odin's son Loki, the fire spirit and mischief-maker among the Æsir.

LOTHURLINGS the people west of the sea (I, chap. 15, 106). The Lothurling flag is a red and black dragon (likely Grengarm) on a wheaten field (II, chap. 38, 455). Presumably the *Western Trader* crosses the ocean to visit their shores, or at least the islands in between.

The Lothurlings are analogous to the Chinese. Able's sword-like mace Sword Breaker, said to be a weapon of the Lothurlings, turns out to be based on a real class of weapons from China. Lothurling characters include Smiler, Stonebowl, and Ironmouth. They call their nation "Realm of the Dragon." Their warrior prince is "Son of the Dragon." The people are "Children of the Dragon." Grengarm is the dragon, and it seems likely that Lothur is "the Fox" (II, chap. 37, 449).

LUD one of Marder's knights, he was badly wounded when they jumped Able (I, chap. 33, 204).
Onomastics: (English) mythic name.

LUT the smith who forged Battlemaid (I, chap. 4, 42).
Myth: (Norse) "stooped," one of the children of Thrall and Thyr. Together Lut and his siblings are the progenitors of the race of slaves. Or Lut is a giant slain by Thor.

LYNNET Etela's mother, a tall woman (II, chap. 21, 241; met in II, chap. 17, 191; named in II, chap. 21, 252). Leesha was her sister and

Kirsten was probably a beloved servant who died. Her house's motto is "marigolds and manticores" (as "manticores and marigolds" II, chap. 17, 195; II, chap. 21, 244). She says there was a ghost where she used to live and he took care of the house but not the people (II, chap. 17, 196). Thiazi says a terrible rage burns in her (II, chap. 21, 257). She is frightening, whipping the eyes of giants, when she shouts her motto. In the Room of Lost Loves she revisits Goldenlawn (II, chap. 22, 259).

Arthuriana: a character who first appears in Malory's "Tale of Sir Gareth of Orkney" where she comes to Arthur's court to find a champion to rescue her sister, Lyones.

Onomastics: Lynet means "bird" (Anglo-Saxon), "grace" (Celtic), "mild" (Latin); Lynnette means "little lion" (French).

M

MAG Bold Berthold's mother, whom he says died before Able was weaned (I, chap. 3, 34). Her husband was Black Berthold, headman of their village. A dragon, probably Setr, took her to the Isle of Glas and made her act as a Siren to lure men to their death (II, chap. 22, 264). She grew old there. Knowing that the khimairae would eat her, she caught Setr's poison in a cup, used it as ink to write the letter with a quill, and then drank the remaining poison.

Able sees her in the Room of Lost Love (II, chap. 22, 263). After he tells her about how the children of Aelf become their kings and queens, she says, "You were a king to me, and to your father and your brother also" (265), a strangely Aelf-like attitude.

Mag's ghost rides off of the Isle of Glas with Lynnet. She talks to Able of "her girlhood in America, how she met my father, and how they came to wed" (II, chap. 27, 335). This seems to refer to Mr. Ormsby, but it more likely refers to Black Berthold.

Myth: close to (Irish) Maga, daughter of the love god Aonghus Og, who wed Ross the Red.

Commentary: Mag is somehow connected to Arthur Ormsby's mother in such a way that she is either the same woman or a twin living in Mythgarthr. Mag came from Earth and took the name (or was given the name) Mag. Mag married Black Berthold and had two sons, first Bold Berthold and then the real Able, at about the same time in her life as her Earth counterpart had two sons, first Ben and then Arthur.

It seems that Mag is either a "serial mom" who had two boys on Earth and then two boys in Mythgarthr, or she is a clone of an Earth girl, that is, a girl who came from Earth to Mythgarthr and left behind a spirit-twin of herself in the same way that Escan leaves a reflection behind in Aelfrice.

Mag seems to have had a childhood as an American girl. Let's say that at the age of ten she read Tolkien, Baum, or some other fantasy author that provided her entry into Mythgarthr and/or Aelfrice, rather like an Alice in Wonderland or a Dorthy in Oz. (There is a somewhat guarded reference to movie *The Wizard of Oz* in the text; there is also a line about "where is the dream my mother had?") This works for serial mom and clone mom. Mag has some strangely Aelf-like notions, and maybe she picked them up vacationing.

But what if the girl started out in Aelfrice? If she's an Aelf, then there is all that trouble with her reality being unstable on higher levels (i.e., Disiri's problem). On the other hand, the possibility that the girl is the human daughter of King Weland raises all sorts of interesting details. When Weland was usurped, this hypothetical daughter might have escaped to another world: America. And then when that situation became less than ideal, she bolted again to Mythgarthr. This would be a serial mom.

This theory would cover her Aelf-culture side: having lived in Aelfrice during her early childhood, she would be in a perfect position to adopt some Aelf attitudes as her own. It would also explain why the usurpers Setr and Grengarm would be so interested in her: her sons would be rightful heirs to the Fire Aelf throne. In this way she wouldn't be just another pretty face; she would be the key to the kingdom.

It might also be a hint as to why she would gravitate towards hardware/smith husbands (Mr. Ormsby certainly, Black Berthold maybe).

It would shed some light on the Isle of Glas, which initially seems to be a Siren Shoal that has been allowed to fall into disrepair for some reason. But if Mag was key to the kingdom, and Mag refused to marry Setr (just as in the story told by Sha), then it seems fitting that the Isle of Glas was built to be a prison of torment created expressly for her confinement, abandoned after her death.

MAGIC HELM part of Able's loot from Jotunland (II, chap. 28, 350), it was a gift from the giantess Borda (II, chap. 30, 365). The view of Uri and Gylf seems to show things as they really are (365).

MAGNEIS the charger Marder gave to Able (I, chap. 45, 279).
Onomastics: (Latin) "mighty, great" (plural form), used for "mighty kings," for example. There is also a surname.

MANASEN one of Arnthor's own knights. He and Erac escort Able to the dungeon (II, chap. 33, 398).
Arthuriana: Manassen of Gaul, one of Arthur's knights. A friend accused Manassen of sleeping with his wife, and in revenge bound him and threw him down a well to drown. Manassen was saved by Morgan le Fay, who rescued him because he was the cousin of her dead lover, Accalon of Gaul. After drowning his former friend, Manassen delivered a threatening message to Arthur from Morgan.

MANI the big black tomcat who followed Able from the witch's cottage (I, chap. 46, 289; first seen in I, chap. 45, 282). His original owner is Huld, then he belongs to Able, Idnn, and Gilling.
Onomastics: Norse "Moon," a saga name for the father of Ketil.

MARC one of the bravest knights of Thortower (II, chap. 32, 391). He traded insults with an Osterling captain and thus started the River Battle a bit early (II, chap. 40, 469).

Arthuriana: Marc (Mark, Marco), King of Cornwall, the husband in the triangle with Isolde of Ireland and his sister's son Tristan.

MARDER the duke whose duchy becomes Celidon's northernmost after Indign's was dissolved (mentioned in I, chap. 4, 42; met in I, chap. 34, 211). Forcetti is his city, and Sheerwall is his castle.
Onomastics: the word *marder* means marten or weasel; the similar name Marden means "from the valley with the pool."

MARGYGR Morcaine's device, a fanciful representation of her mother, who also bore Setr and Arnthor (II, glossary; II, chap. 32, 388). See also NYKR.
Myth: (Norse) a mermaid or ugly monster.

MEYNARD, YVES a French-Canadian author (born 1964) to whom *The Knight* is dedicated. *The Wizard* begins with a quote from his novel *The Book of Knights* (1998).

The Book of Knights is about a boy named Adelrune who reads a forbidden book, "The Book of Knights," and runs away from home to become a knight. For his quest he aims to free a puppet from her cruel toy maker. He finds his way to a sort of wizard knight named Riander and pays him six years of his life for his training, growing to manhood overnight.

The style and setting are more like Hoffman or Jack Vance than a traditional knightly tale. Obviously the Quixote angle comes into play, too, because of the role a knightly book plays in starting the adventure.

MICE Angrborn name for people who are half Angrborn and half human (I, chap. 10, 76). Heimir and Hela are two examples in the text.

MICHAEL a man from Kleos (I, chap. 44, 275). He summons Valfather to show Able how such summoning is done (276). He comments on Eterne and Zio.

Myth: (Hebrew) one of the few angels named in the Torah, thus thought to be an archangel.
Onomastics: (Hebrew) "who is like God?"

MIRMIR a magic spring (II, chap. 5, 56). "Drinking from it brings back certain forgotten memories" (II, glossary). When Able drinks here he visits himself, watching as he drinks water at Bluestone Castle (I, chap. 2, 24).
Myth: (Norse) Mimir (Mimr, Mimi) is a wise being associated with the World Tree and the Spring of Urth. After being put to death by the Vanir, his head was kept by Odin and consulted as an oracle in times of perplexity.

MODGUD a giantess who guards the Bridge of Swords (II, chap. 24, 294). Her face is naked bone, except for a maiden's eyes (295). See also MODGUDA.
Myth: (Norse) Modgud (or Modudr) is the maiden who kept the bridge on the road to Hel. Hermod meets her there on his mission to the land of the dead.

MODGUDA a serving woman in Sheerwall Castle (I, chap. 33, 204). She tends to Able during his recovery there from near death. Her name is very close to that of Modgud.

MONEY
farthing—copper coin (I, chap. 16, 109).
scield—silver coin. Twenty-four to a sceptre (II, chap. 33, 400). One month's wages for sailor or stableman (I, chap. 18, 118).
sceptre—gold coin (I, chap. 15, 102).

MONGAN see SPELL OF DIVINATION.

MOONRIDER any knight the Lady sends to Mythgarthr (I, chap. 21, 133). Able sees one and Kerl says Nur can see them at times (133).

MOONRISE Svon's mount (II, chap. 2, 24).

MORCAINE a woman first mentioned by Garsecg as being his sister (I, chap. 22, 140) but turns out later to be the princess whom Able first meets as a human sacrifice set out for Grengarm by some Aelf, Uri among them. Morcaine is second born, between Setr and Arnthor. She travels via shadows to meet Able at Redhall (II, chap. 28, 341). She says Able stabbed Gilling (342). She is Duchess of Ringwood (II, chap. 33, 395). She says Able is dead, that the Valkyrie's kiss did it (II, chap. 34, 405). Because he is dead she claims power over him, since her magic is necromantic (406). Her device is a margygr. The magic helm shows she has a serpent body below the waist.
Arthuriana: Morgaine or Morgan le Fay, a sister to Arthur.

MORI a smith in Irringsmouth, he sells Able Sword Breaker, the sword-like mace (I, chap. 15, 103).
Onomastics: (German) Möri, nickname of Morhart (hardy, brave, strong); a word meaning "my teacher" in the Yemenite Jewish tradition; and also a Latin word for "death/die," as in *memento mori* (remember you must die).

MOSS AELF Disiri's clan (I, chap. 7, 58). The only Aelf clan ruled by a queen (II, chap. 32, 382).

MOSSMAIDENS girls of the Moss Aelf (I, chap. 7, 57).

MOSSMATRONS older women of the Moss Aelf (I, glossary only).

MOSSMEN men of the Moss Aelf (I, chap. 3, 35).

MOST HIGH GOD the single inhabitant of the first level, Elysion. To look upon his face is lethal for humans (II, chap. 20, 234).

MOST LOW GOD the single inhabitant of the seventh level, Niflheim (II, chap. 31, 373).

MOTHER Able says of his mother, "she was still a young girl, not a great deal older than Sha, when she went away" (I, chap. 51, 319). Sha herself is probably the same age as her husband Scaur, who is "not a lot older" than Able himself (I, chap. 2, 25), at a time when he thought himself a teen.

MOUNTAIN OF FIRE seemingly a volcano in Mythgarthr; a gateway to Muspel (I, chap. 28, 177). Garsecg mentions the Osterlings sacrificed to Setr when they held it (I, chap. 25, 162). Thunrolf has Pouk thrown in, then chains himself to Able to go after Pouk.

MOUNTAINS OF THE MICE the name the giants use for Mountains of the North, because the half-giant "mice" live there.

MOUNTAINS OF THE NORTH the mountains between Celidon and Jotunland (I, chap. 13, 89).

MOUNTAINS OF THE SUN the mountains between Celidon and Osterland (I, chap. 13, 89).

MUSPEL the world of the sixth level, under Aelfrice, where the dragons come from (I, chap. 6, 52). See COSMOLOGY.
Myth: (Norse) Muspell (two Ls) is the realm of fire, the heat from which helped in the creation of the world. The sons of Muspell, Fire Giants, ride out against the gods at Ragnarok.

MYSTERY OF KING GILLING'S MURDER Gilling arranges a battle between randomly selected giants and the best champions among the knights. The resulting battle sets Bittergarm and Skoel against Garvaon and Svon. Before the fight, Gilling kills the herald Crol, enraging Svon (II, chap. 12, 138). During the fight there is interference by spectator giants (139). An invisible or dark being starts putting out the lights (141). A tall woman (Huld, Uri, or Baki) arrives, impersonating a giantess (141). Then someone stabs Gilling in the back. This is the first attack. He is struck again later, when he rises from his sickbed (II, chap. 20, 245). The second attack is not necessarily by the same person who made the first attack.

Suspects (in order of appearance)

- Toug, because he goes into a weird frenzy and wants to kill Gilling at about the time it happens. The witch Huld and Mani suspect him (II, chap. 14, 157–58). Idnn and Beel suspect him (II, chap. 25, 309–10).
- Org, because he might have put out the lights. Toug seems to have seen Org killing a giant (141), but it wasn't Gilling. Pouk suspects Org (II, chap. 12, 142). Mani doubts. Org claims innocence (II, chap. 25, 308).
- Baki, because Uri tells Able that Baki did it (II, chap. 13, 147). Able hints that Baki would do it to save Toug (149).
- The Valfather is an unnamed suspect. The Overcyns are known for their fights against giants. The Valfather, as lord of hosts, might be especially angered by Gilling's ill treatment of his guests, including the killing of their herald. Uri is about to tell Idnn who did it when suddenly the Valfather shows up.
- Idnn is a suspect. She swears she didn't do it (II, chap. 14, 161). She fears it was a blind man (164), presumably meaning Pouk or Vil.
- Uri proclaims her innocence (II, chap. 20, 234).
- The two-headed giant Orgalmir/Borgalmir. Able uses him as an example, saying Orgalmir struck the first blow, and Borgalmir struck the second (II, chap. 21, 253). There may be more truth to this than originally intended, in that the killer may have been two of one, somehow.
- Svon claims innocence (II, chap. 25, 312).
- Garvaon seems to confess (II, chap. 26, 324).
- Able is suspected by Morcaine (II, chap. 28, 342).
- Schildstarr is suspected by Wistan (II, chap. 30, 362).

MYTHGARTHR a world on the fourth level, the world that belongs to humans, where Celidon is located (I, chap. 2, 24; I, chap. 3, 31). For other nations see FIVE REALMS. See also COSMOLOGY. Other worlds on the fourth level include Dream, Earth, and possibly Hel.
Myth: (Norse) Midgard or Midgarthr, the world of men, midway between the gods and the giants.

N

NAMES ON THE WIND Able hears a list of names on the wind, presumably Disiri's former lovers (I, chap. 67, 412). In addition to both of his names, he hears:

- Walewein—Middle Dutch Gawain, hero of Arthurian cycle. See GAWAIN.
- Wace—(circa A.D. 1115–circa 1183) Anglo-Norman poet of Arthuriana.
- Vortigern—semi-legendary king of Britain, who set the stage for Arthur.
- Kyot—mysterious French poet who supplied source of Parzival to Wolfram von Eschenbach. See SVON.
- Yvain—knight of the Round Table.
- Gottfried—Gottfried von Strassburg (died circa A.D. 1210), German poet, Tristan and Isolde.
- Eilhart—Eilhart von Oberge, German poet of late 12th century, known for earliest form of Tristan and Isolde.
- Palamedes—Knight of the Round Table, a Saracen convert.

- Duach—one of Arthur's warriors.
- Tristan—Knight of the Round Table.
- Albrecht—Albrecht von Scharfenberg, 13th century author who expanded a fragment by Wolfram von Eschenbach into "Younger Titurel," with over 6300 verses.
- Caradoc—Knight of the Round Table, semi-legendary ancestor to the kings of Gwent.

NASTROND Able was at the siege of Nastrond during his twenty years in Skai, but Escan has never heard of the place (I, chap. 35, 414).
Myth: (Norse) Nastrand ("corpse-strand"), a bad place after Ragnarok, but not the worst, which is Hvergelmir.

NEEDAM an island south of Celidon (I, chap. 28, 177). Able has never been there. Kerl reports that the *Western Trader* was "stove off Needam, and laid up seven weeks for repair" (177).
Onomastics: the name Needam is part of the ancient Anglo-Saxon legacy of Britain, with places in Derbyshire, Norfolk, and Suffolk, and became a surname for its residents.

NERTHIS an Overcyn who lives in Mythgarthr as the queen of wild animals (II, chap. 3, 35). She makes trees grow.
Myth: (Norse) Nerthus, fertility goddess worshipped in Denmark in the first century A.D., as described by Tacitus. The mother of Freyja, the Lady, by some accounts.

NIFLHEIM the lowest world, where the Most Low God is (II, chap. 35, 419–22). See COSMOLOGY.
Myth: (Norse) the abode of darkness, beneath the roots of the World Tree.

NJORS a sailor on the *Western Trader* (I, chap. 20, 127).
Onomastics: probably from the Old Norse Njordr, god of sailing, whose name means "strong, vigorous."

NOLAA servant of Svon's father, she and her husband raised Svon (II, chap. 19, 230).
Onomastics: perhaps the Celtic name Nola, short form of Finnula, meaning "white shouldered."

NOPEL a knight of Duke Marder whose device is pards (II, chap. 11, 126). The pard is a great cat, the cheetah or the panther: in medieval times, the leopard was thought to be a hybrid of lion and pard.
Onomastics: the name appeared in the Plauen area of Germany in the 15th century but the meaning remains unknown.
Commentary: the great cats are represented in Celidon's heraldry with Ravd (lion), Leort (leopard), and Nopel (pard).

NORN-HOUND Ulfa's word for a wolf? (I, chap. 8, 63).

NORTHHOLDING the manor of Sir Loth when he was alive (II, chap. 32, 389).

NOTT a giantess (II, chap. 16, 183). "She is one of the nicer Giants of Winter and Old Night. Night in Mythgarthr belongs to her" (II, glossary). See also AUD.
Myth: (Norse) Nott is the personification of Night in the Poetic Edda.

NUKARA mother of Uns and Duns (I, chap. 38, 234). She is killed when Osterlings raid her farm (II, chap. 37, 438).
Myth: (Egyptian) a foreign goddess based on the Babylonian Ningal (male deity of the underworld).

NUR the second mate on the *Western Trader* (I, chap. 16, 108).
Onomastics: (Arabic) name meaning "light."
Myth: (Babylonian) Nur-Dagan, one of three kings to have crossed the Sea of Death. The other two were Utnapishtim and Sargon.

NYKIR KING OF ARMS the title of King Arnthor's herald (II, chap. 30, 361).

NYKR creature (I, chap. 4, 43) depicted on the shield on the back of a coin: "a monster compounded of woman, horse, and fish" (38). It appears on the flag of Celidon. See also MARGYGR.
Myth: (Norse) "river horse," which leads to the German *nixie,* a creature with a human torso and fish tail.

NYTIR the knight whom Able bests at the Dollop and Scallop (I, chap. 35, 225). Nytir of Fairhall, his arms are a ram (I, chap. 37, 229). He has a house in Forcetti (I, chap. 36, 226). Nytir's squire tells Able that he was one of those who pummeled Able on the practice field (226). This implies that Nytir did, too, and was hunting Able to finish the job.
Onomastics: Icelandic word for "(a number of) uses," functions or purposes for which something may be employed. In this sense linked to both Able and Toug.

OBR Svon's father, a baron (I, chap. 48, 300).
Onomastics: Czech name meaning "giant, titan."

OLAFR one of Svon's brother's men-at-arms (II, chap. 1, 27).
Onomastics: (Old Norse) heir. See LEIFR, LORD.

OLD TOUG father of Ulfa and Toug (I, chap. 6, 51). He is the first to see Able after the boy has been transformed into a man, and he laughs in shock and surprise at Able's naked condition (I, chap. 8, 59). Able demands clothing, so he takes him home and has Ulfa sew a shirt and trousers. Old Toug, Vali, and Toug try to ambush Able but he beats the men and chases the boy (64). He and Toug take a trip to Aelfrice where Disiri borrows the boy.

Weeks later Able sets out to hunt the outlaws. He meets old Toug again to question him (I, chap. 12, 84). Old Toug volunteers to lead Able to the place. Together they kill many, and old Toug is moved by how well Able treats him. They divide the loot from the outlaw cave.

OLOF the baron who took over the Mountain of Fire while Thunrolf and Able were in Muspel (I, chap. 31, 192). He gives Able a present of an Osterling knife having silver hilt and scabbard, both set with coral (195). Able gives this to Kerl.
Onomastics: Norse word meaning "relic/ancient."

ORG the ogre that Able got from Uns (I, chap. 40, 247). "He was a man-shaped snake but hot instead of cold, but he was really more like a gorilla" (I, glossary). Toug believes Org was extinguishing the torches just before Gilling was struck (II, chap. 14, 158–59).

ORGALMIR the left head of Schildstarr's two-headed friend (II, chap. 21, 253). He is in the group trying to ambush the human party after they have left Utgard (II, chap. 23, 282). In the ensuing fight, Able tries to sweep both heads off, but he only gets one. See BORGALMIR.

ORIEL one of the five brave knights who stay in the area to the end of Able's fight against Loth (II, chap. 32, 391).
Arthuriana: a Saxon king who invaded northern Britain at the beginning of Arthur's reign, his name is an Old German compound of "fire" and "war/battle/strife."

ORMSBY, ARTHUR the boy from America who narrates the story (II, chap. 40, 477). He had a Macintosh computer in America (I, chap. 9, 73). The god Michael says Arthur's MOTHER never knew Arthur (I, chap. 44, 274). She left soon after he was born, still a young woman. Arthur's brother is Ben. Arthur's FATHER had a hardware store. He died when Arthur was very young, and Ben raised his little brother in the house, most likely with their GRANDMOTHER there.

Legend says that in A.D. 840, Orm the Viking, a youngest son, went to England and conquered a spot of Lancashire called Ormskirk, "dragon church." About a thousand years later, John Ormsby (1829–1895) was a British translator most famous for his 1885 version of *Don Quixote*.
Onomastics: Ormsby is either "elm-place" (orm) or "snake-place" (orme).

The latter is interesting because of Arnthor's presumed half-snake body (if he is like his sister). It might also be a code: orms/by = by Orm, meaning "near-Worm," i.e., "pen-Dragon."

OSSAR Disira's baby (I, chap. 9, 72). First alluded to as "Seaxneat's wife's new baby" (I, chap. 4, 38). Able gives him to a Bodachan couple (I, chap. 11, 80).
Myth: (Irish) "the hound of Mac Da Tho that was coveted by Ailill and Medb and also by Conchobhar Mac Nessa. In another version, the hound is called Ailbe. At the end of the story of Mac Da Tho's Boar, the dog chases Ailill's chariot and is killed by his charioteer" (Ellis).

OSTERLAND the country east of the Mountains of the Sun (I, chap. 5, 49), Öster being Germanic for "east." The Osterling pirates follow the coast from Osterland "south, west, and north, murdering and stealing. Duke Indign had tried to stop them, but they had killed him, and pulled down his castle" (I, chap. 16, 111). This implies an Osterling Sea.

OSTERLINGS the inhabitants of Osterland, a people who eat other people to become more human (I, chap. 19, 123). They worship the dragons of Muspel, sacrificing humans to them directly when they hold the Mountain of Fire. Their culture seems to be a blend of Middle-Eastern elements (Khazneh, spahis) and Mongolian elements (caan).

OVERCYNS the people of Skai: the Valfather's people. "Nobody calls the Overcyns gods" (I, chap. 44, 274). "We obeyed the Overcyns, mostly, only when we were afraid we could not get away with not obeying" (I, chap. 45, 280). The first generation of Overcyns were people from Kleos who descended to Skai to kill the primordial giant Ymir, with the understanding that they would not be allowed back in Kleos. Thus their brothers in Kleos have become their gods in Skai (II, chap. 4, 46–47).

Included among the Overcyns are

- Bragi—god of poetry, consort to Idnn. Mentioned in spell to turn ghosts visible.
- Forcetti—god of law, Forseti. Probably second (or third) generation, being son of Baldr in Norse myth.
- Frigg—fertility goddess, she is the Valfather's queen and mother of Thunor. First generation.
- Idnn—Idun, guardian of the apples of youth. Second generation Overcyn, since she seems to be sister to the Lady.
- the Lady—Freyja. Second generation, youngest daughter of the Valfather.
- Ler—sea god (Celtic, not Æsir).
- Lothur—the name of Odin's brother (first generation), but this character is said to be the youngest son of the Valfather (second generation).
- Nerthis—fertility goddess who lives in Mythgarthr.
- Ran—sea goddess.
- Sif—Thunor's wife. Probably second generation.
- Thunor—god of thunder, Thor. Second generation Overcyn, son of the Valfather.
- Tyr—god of justice.
- the Valfather—king of the Overcyns, Odin. First generation.

Onomastics: possibly "high family," since Old English *cyn* means "kin."
Myth: (Norse) they are largely equivalent to the Æsir, the family of gods in Asgard.

OWAN a knight who had died (II, chap. 29, 352). His wife, a Dame, then married a draper. After this second husband died, she wished to resume her title but the neighbors were against it.
Arthuriana: Owain, son of Urien.
Onomastics: (Welsh) Owein, Owen, Owin, Owain, meaning "young warrior."

PALAMEDES see NAMES ON THE WIND.

PAPOUNCE one of Beel's upper servants, in charge of the other servants (I, chap. 47, 293).
Onomastics: Scott Wowra wonders if it might be a playful "papa ounce," or "father cat," perhaps alluding to his cat-herding of the servants.

PARKA the woman from Kleos who gave Able his bowstring (I, chap. 1, 21). Her cave is between Aelfrice and Mythgarthr (I, chap. 2, 24). Her work with the string (spinning, measuring, and cutting) recalls the three Fates, and the string itself seems to be made up of lives, furthering this association. Parka names him, and when he resists, she penalizes him: "The lower your lady the higher your love" and "You shall sink before you rise, and rise before you sink" (21). Able meets her again through the Room of Lost Loves (II, chap. 22, 261).
Myth: (Latin) Parca, mythic name for the Furies.

Commentary: Norse mythology is very clear that the Æsir have no power over Fate. Wolfe incorporates this by having Fate come from a higher world.

PAYN the Earl Marshal's chief clerk (II, chap. 29, 354). He is the bastard son of Escan, the Earl Marshal, by way of Wiliga, maid of Escan's mother (II, chap. 36, 431).
Onomastics: Payne means "rustic" (Latin), "pagan" (English).

PHOLSUNG a former king of Celidon, grandfather of Beel and Arnthor (I, chap. 48, 298; 302).

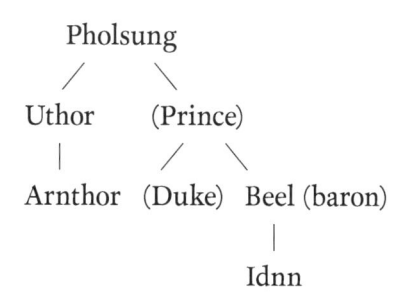

```
                Pholsung
                /      \
           Uthor       (Prince)
             |          /    \
         Arnthor  (Duke)   Beel (baron)
                              |
                            Idnn
```

Myth: (Norse) Phol perhaps is Vol, thought to be a fertility god.

POTASH teacher of chemistry and physics in America (I, chap. 7, 56).

POUK BADEYE a sailor Able hired at Irringsmouth (I, chap. 15, 102). Able says his age is around twenty when they are near the pass (I, chap. 50, 314). After Able left him the last time, Pouk was important. "He was Master Pouk then, and worked for the king" (I, chap. 31, 197). Ah, but who is the king after Arnthor?
Onomastics: Shakespeare's Puck, from Middle English *pouk* (evil spirit, puck, goblin) and perhaps Norwegian Puk (a water sprite).

QUEEN OF THE WOOD another name for Disiri (I, chap. 9, 73).

QUIXOTE see DON QUIXOTE.

QUT the leader of the men-at-arms at Redhall (II, chap. 27, 337). His name "sounds southern," and in fact his mother was from the south. *Onomastics:* Old Turkish word meaning "princely charisma," "grace of heaven," "blessing." (Found carved on a stone in runic script.)

R

RAN a sea goddess known to sailors (I, chap. 17, 115).
Myth: Norse wife of Ægir, the sea-deity. Her name means "plunder." She drew seafaring men down to herself in the depths. See AEGRI'S ISLE for possible connection.

RAVD the best knight Able ever saw (I, chap. 4, 38). He had been Sabel's squire for 12 years, which suggests that he was at least 24 when he was knighted. He pays Able to guide him through the woods to Glennidam. His shield shows a gold lion with bloody claws (I, chap. 8, 60). Toug thinks his name means "ravisher" (61). Redhall is his manor. The outlaws near Glennidam kill him. Years later and many leagues away, Squire Toug sees a spectral knight near Sir Svon at Utgard, with a golden lion rampant on his helm and a gold lion on his shield, but Svon doesn't see it (II, chap. 19, 230–31).
Onomastics: likely a variant of the Norse name Raud, meaning "red." (Note that Ravd's manor is Redhall and his shield's lion has red claws.) Historically, there was a Raud in Northern Norway who, as a

worshiper of red-bearded Thor, was put to death by Olaf Tryggvason (Davidson). See also ROWD.

REAL ABLE, THE the brother of Bold Berthold, whom Disiri switched with Arthur. Bold Berthold in Jotunhome says that Able was taken from Mythgarthr, was gone for many years, but returned the same age as when he had left (I, chap. 66, 403). Mag tells of how her son the real Able visited her on the Isle of Glas.

The real Able is probably in America, taking Arthur Ormsby's place. Sir Able has a number of dream-like episodes that might be snippets of the real Able's experience there. In one, he wakes up searching for a machine gun (I, chap. 19, 122); in another, he wakes up in a hospital, a hero who saved a plane from hijackers (125); in a third, he thinks about "how I used to live in a place where there were swords and no cars" (I, chap. 20, 133). Most chillingly, there is the dream-vision of the crowded highway where Sir Able sees an ambulance and knows that the real Able is in it, and he wants to help him, but he cannot (II, chap. 38, 459). It seems as though the real Able in America joined the military, became a hero against hijackers, and likely met his end in that ambulance after another heroic act.

Onomastics: obviously the name is an indicator of ability, but it also has a haunting link to Abel, the younger brother of Cain. Abel was a shepherd, Cain was a farmer, and God seemed to favor Abel's sacrifices more than Cain's sacrifices, so Cain killed Abel. (Another tradition has it that a woman was involved. This forms a tenuous link to Geri.) A further intriguing detail is that the name Cain might come from an Arabic word for "smith" (and *The Wizard Knight* is rich with smith-related mythology). Still, even though Bold Berthold has a mysterious head wound that might be a "mark of Cain," there is no indication that he killed the real Able. Besides, since Able does not really become "Arthur" in Mythgarthr, there is little reason to suppose that the real Able in America would suffer the fate of Abel.

REALM OF THE DRAGON the Lothurling's name for their empire (II, chap. 38, 453).

RED TIJANAMIR the old Caan's first-born son, whose fate foretold was that he would reign but die young, crushed by a stone. At the death of his father, he became the new caan. Shortly thereafter he removed his helm to wipe his brow and a slingstone killed him (II, chap. 37, 443).

REDHALL Ravd's manor (I, chap. 4, 38). It is located on the War Way and its neighbor is Goldenlawn. Duke Marder promises it to Able (II, chap. 23, 288). From Redhall to Kingsdoom is more than one week of travel for Able's group (Gylf, Wistan, Pouk, and Uns), but Able, Cloud, and Gylf could have covered it in one hour (II, chap. 28, 348).

RIVER BATTLE the climactic battle where Able calls up Aelf archers and Arnthor kills the Black Caan with the Aelf sword (II, chap. 40, 469).

RIVER ROAD the main road inland from Irringsmouth (I, chap. 2, 26). It runs along the north bank of the Irring.

ROBER OF GREENGLORY the fourth knight bested by Able at halberts (II, chap. 30, 369). He is among the five who stay through to the end of Able's fight against Loth (II, chap. 32, 391), and he later fights alongside Able at the River Battle.
Onomastics: (French) modern form of Robert, meaning "bright fame."

ROOM OF LOST LOVE "a room that was like another world when you got inside. Sometimes dead people were alive again in there" (II, glossary). A room in Thiazi's section of Utgard (first mentioned in I, chap. 31, 197; later visited in II, chap. 21, 257).

ROUND TOWER the biggest castle at the Mountain of Fire (I, chap. 29, 179).

ROWD a slave of Logi later owned by Svon (II, chap. 23, 277). The "sound man" (II, chap. 21, 251), he was paired to Gif.
Onomastics: probably from the Old Norse name Raud meaning "red." See also RAVD.

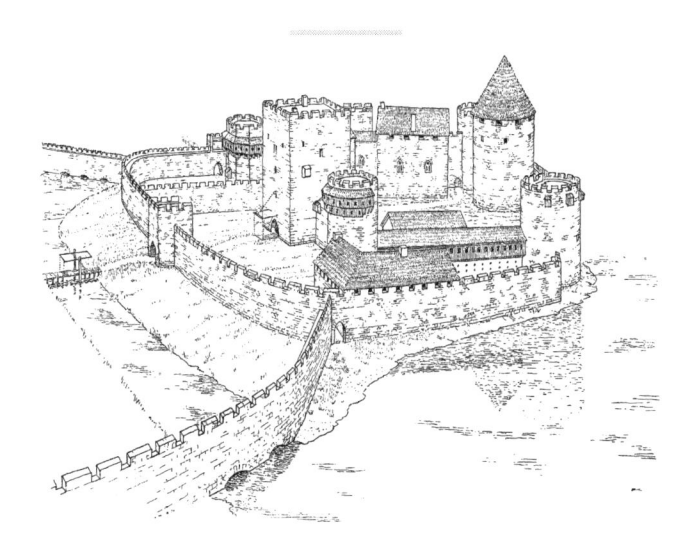

SABEL a dead knight, Ravd had been his squire for twelve years (I, chap. 5, 45). Sabel beat Ravd twice. Once with the flat of his sword because Ravd attacked him. Once with his hands because of something said or not said; Sabel was drunk at the time.
Onomastics: Dutch/German word for "sabre"; also a homonym for sable, the color black in heraldry.

SALAMANDERS the Fire Aelf (I, chap. 3, 35). Uri and Baki are Salamanders.

SANDHILL CASTLE a manor belonging to Leort's father, it is located far down on the southern border of Celidon (II, chap. 9, 99).

SCATTER OF THE DRAGON'S BLOOD Smiler's term for Able, as a liegelord or a godling: "You, Scatter of the Dragon's Blood, are my ultimate ancestor, but let us have also the blessing of the Fox" (II, chap. 39, 465).

SCAUR a friendly fisherman in Irringsmouth, who is not much older than newly arrived Able (I, chap. 2, 25). He brings Able to the mainland from Bluestone Island. His wife is Sha. He tells a scary ghost story. Sha's grandfather lives with them.
Onomastics: Scottish word, from the Icelandic *sker*, a skerry, for an isolated rock in the sea; later applied to a protruding rock, rocky eminence, or bare place on the side of a mountain. Mentioned in Tennyson's "Bugle Song" from *The Princess:* "O sweet and far, from cliff and scaur, The horns of Elfland faintly blowing."

SCEEF Logi's slave, paired to Alca (II, chap. 23, 277).
Onomastics: close to Saxon legendary first king Sceaf, who in one legend is a child who came over the sea to rule Denmark, and in another legend is a son of Noah.

SCHILDSTARR one of the most important Agrborn, mentioned by Bold Berthold as the leader of the raid on Griffinsford (I, chap. 2, 28; met in II, chap. 12, 135). He weighs two tons (II, chap. 15, 169). After Gilling dies, Schildstarr becomes the new king (II, chap. 22, 266). Later he is killed by Bold Berthold.

SEAGIRT Thunrolf's castle (I, chap. 31, 192). The name implies that it is on the coast.

SEAXNEAT a man in Glennidam who trades with the outlaws (I, chap. 4, 38). His wife is Disira; their baby is Ossar. He is tall, fat, red-bearded, and pigeon-toed (I, chap. 6, 53).
Myth: (Anglo-Saxon) "sword companion," a god worshipped by the Old Saxons and remembered as ancestor of the kings of Essex.

SETR a dragon with a human father (I, chap. 9, 69). His sister is Morcaine; his brother is Arnthor. He was first born and his mother kept him close (II, chap. 34, 409). He nearly took over Aelfrice, enlisting the Fire Aelf and building the Tower of Glas, but Able is sure that what he really wanted was to conquer Mythgarthr (II, glossary).

He controls the Sea Aelf and he often goes by the watery name of Garsecg. He is resisted by the other Aelf clans. See also SURT.

Setr might be in two places at once: the dragon in Muspel met by Able and Thunrolf is Setr, who was last seen as Garsecg, dividing his time between Aelfrice and Mythgarthr. Or maybe Setr/Garsecg just goes there for dinner.
Myth: (Norse) Surt or Surtr, a Fire Giant from Muspell who burns earth and heaven; (Egyptian) Set, evil brother of Osiris and Isis.

SEVENGATES Escan's castle (II, chap. 36, 425), located five days east of Kingsdoom—or three days if one hurries (428).

SHA a fishwife who is nice to Able at Irringsmouth (I, chap. 2, 25). Her husband is Scaur. She is probably the woman in Irringsmouth who told the story "about a girl who was supposed to get married to an Aelf king and she cheated him out of her bed" (I, chap. 3, 30).
Onomastics: possibly Gaelic "Shae" (from the fairy fort; fairy palace).

SHA'S GRANDFATHER tells Able about spiny orange trees (I, chap. 2, 25).

SHEERWALL Duke Marder's castle, near Forcetti (I, chap. 32, 198; seen in I, chap. 42, 259). It is a league away from the port city, at a stronger place (II, chap. 28, 348) to the east (I, chap. 41, 255). Among its structures are the Marshal's Tower (for Master Agr) and the Duchess's Tower.

SIF Thunor's wife (II, chap. 3, 36).
Myth: (Norse) Thor's second wife, with wonderful golden hair.

SIRONA see SPELL OF DIVINATION.

SKAI the third world, above Mythgarthr, where the Overcyns are (I, chap. 3, 31).

SKATHI a giantess of Winter and Old Night (II, chap. 24, 293).
Myth: (Norse) a giantess. A "snowshoe goddess," she is counted among the Æsir.

SKJALDMEYJAR the female giants (II, chap. 36, 434).
Onomastics: (Norse) shield-maidens.

SKJENA a girl who lived in Griffinsford (I, chap. 3, 34). Daughter of Uld, she had six fingers.
Onomastics: probably "skittish, shy." Norwegian *skjena* means "to run off because of mosquitoes" (of cows); Swedish *skena* and Jutish *skjenne* mean "to shy" (of a horse).

SKOEL one of two giants (the other is Bitergarm) randomly selected to fight the knights in Gilling's hall (II, chap. 12, 137). Svon fights Skoel and wounds the giant's hand. The giants think they have won, but the men rally to press the fight. Svon and Garvaon together kill Skoel just before Gilling is struck (II, chap. 14, 166).
Onomastics: possibly the wolf that chases the sun, SKOLL, which see.

SKOGSALFAR learned term for Mossmen (II, chap. 39, 465).
Onomastics: Norse *skog* is "forest," so the word means "forest elf."

SKOLL the last knight to bear Eterne before Able (II, chap. 9, 98). He was killed by Grengarm. The mail he wore, found by Able, is blessed. Every fifth ring is gold. This sounds like Beowulf's armor (see WELAND).
Myth: (Norse) "treachery," the wolf that chases the sun through the sky every day. Son of Fenrir.

SMILER the Celidonian term for He Who Smiles, the Dragon Prince (II, chap. 38, 452). "The dragon was Grengarm. His people were Lothurlings" (II, glossary).

SNARI the villager of Griffinsford who fed the old man who had told them the Aelf had cursed them (II, chap. 22, 264). The old man spoke of Grengarm, but he was himself Grengarm, or perhaps Setr.
Onomastics: Old West Norse name and nickname meaning "fast, rash, hasty; sharp."

SON OF THE BLOOD OF THE SKAI DRAGON Smiler's title after he follows Able (II, chap. 39, 464).

SON OF THE DRAGON the title for a warrior prince of the Lothurlings (II, chap. 38, 452). Two royal brothers fight. The loser gets the father's throne; the winner gets the glory of expanding the Realm of the Dragon. The Talking Table tells him which direction to go: north, south, or west, since east is ocean.
Myth: in China, the emperor is the human incarnation of the dragon god.

SOUTHERN REALM a generic term for the unnamed kingdom south of Celidon, beyond the Greenflood River. This region is the source of the name Qut, and home to the herdsman and his family (II, chap. 39, 460–61). It is probably one of the five realms represented by coins in Able's loot from Jotunland.

It seems that Smiler's group landed here after sailing over from the land of the Lothurlings. According to Stonebowl, they captured five towns, all well stocked, "and had taken the coast road only after gaining food enough to carry them to next spring" (II, chap. 38, 455). Smiler aims to carve out his kingdom in the south, and Arnthor has sworn to help him in that (456).

SPAHIS Osterling warriors (II, chap. 40, 473).
History: knights of the Ottoman Empire (Ottoman Turkish word *sipahi*, from Persian *sepah*, meaning "army").

SPARREO Able's math teacher in America (I, chap. 4, 41).

SPELL OF DIVINATION in Beel's attempt at finding what happened to Pouk and Ulfa, he calls out a spell listing three names (I, chap. 59, 362):

- Mongan—an Irish hero.
- Dirmaid—one of the Irish Fenians, a group exterminated in A.D. 277.
- Sirona—continental Celtic goddess, also known as "Dirona" (and possibly "Tsirona"). A healing goddess, whose name means "star." Frequently depicted with serpents and eggs (Monaghan).

SPELL TO TURN GHOSTS VISIBLE Able reads this spell, a list of five names, out of an Aelf book in Escan's library (II, chap. 29, 354).

- Mannanan—Celtic sea god, riding over the sea in a chariot.
- Mider—Celtic god of the underworld.
- Bragi—Norse god of poetry, consort to goddess Idnn.
- Boe—son of Odin and Rind, he avenged Balder's death by killing Hoder.
- Llyr—Welsh sea god, father of Manannan. Same as Irish god Lir.

SPINY ORANGE the tree much revered by the Moss Aelf, such that they have their revenge upon those who cut one down.

There are a few enigmas about this. In the first place, when Able breaks a branch off in America or Mythgarthr, it seems to act in a negative way as a "Golden Bough" in allowing him to enter Aelfrice, where he is treated roughly for messing with the tree. To make up for his transgression, Able plants three spiny orange seeds, yet later he has no qualms about taking spiny orange branches to make arrows. Thus, despite his memory of taking only a branch, it seems that he must have cut down an entire tree for his six-foot staff, which seems like a very small tree. Otherwise, his persecution by the Moss Aelf was disproportionate, since he only took a branch.

In the ruins of Griffinsford, Bold Berthold shows Able where the real Able had planted a seed before he left. There is a stump, which they mourn, but at the edge of the field is a 25-foot-tall spiny orange tree. It is ambiguous as to which one was planted by the real Able (in fact, maybe this presentation amounted to a test of Able by Bold Berthold). Aside from that, there is a haunting sense that Able must have cut down the other one: that is, the stump belongs to the tree that is now his bow.

Much later, when Sir Able is preparing to hold the mountain pass, he rides off on Cloud one night and returns with a lance made of spiny orange. It seems like this must be one of the two in Bold Berthold's field, either the tall one, or the former tree of the stump, but the latter requires some troubling time travel. If it is the tall one, perhaps Able cuts it knowing that he has already paid for it (by planting the seeds before).

STONEBOWL one of Smiler's chief ministers, the one with the dragon-shaped sword (met in II, chap. 38, 452; named on 455).

SURT the helper of ship's cook Hordsvin on the *Western Trader* (I, chap. 19, 125). Both men fight beside Able against the Osterling pirates. Able never meets him. The similarity of his name to that of Setr seems like a smoking gun, leaving an impression that Able's grievous wound, in his side, might have come from Surt on behalf of Setr. *Myth:* (Norse) Surt or Surtr, the most famous named giant: a Fire Giant from Muspell who burns earth and heaven.

SVON Ravd's squire (I, chap. 4, 37), later Able's squire (I, chap. 43, 269). Obr is his father and he has an older brother. Able leaves him in the forest because he is afraid he would kill Svon (I, chap. 44, 273). Svon quarrels with Pouk and goes south, followed by Org. He meets a Mouse and gives him a gift, but the half-giant comes back at night and keeps hanging around until Org kills him. Spooked by Org, Svon heads north, passing Lady Idnn and getting into the fight with Toug wherein Toug breaks Svon's nose with a sucker punch (II, chap. 2, 23).

Svon starts to remember the outlaw attack in which Ravd died (II, chap. 1, 28). His shield bears the image of a swan (II, chap. 12, 133). He marries Queen Idnn, who has become very enamored of him.
Arthuriana: the Knight of the Swan is a figure of Chivalric Romance, a mysterious rescuer who comes in a swan-drawn boat to defend a damsel. Originally attached to the family of Godfrey of Bouillon and the Crusade Cycle, in Wolfram von Eschenbach's *Parzival* the Swan Knight is Lohengrin, son of the Grail knight Percival. This version is the source of Wagner's opera *Lohengrin,* the most famous Swan Knight today.
Commentary: Svon's initial problem is his bad attitude. Toug teaches him humility by breaking his nose in their fight, or perhaps through Toug's behavior after the fight, and this seems to go a long way in helping Svon's personality mature so that he becomes closer to an ideal knight. It is ironic, because a beating from Ravd or Able, which Svon had been so actively seeking, would probably not have had the same salubrious effect.

SWERT Beel's valet, whom Beel orders to verbally abuse Able (I, chap. 61, 373). He does so, reluctantly. He comes to Able after the Battle of Utgard to bring him to Beel (II, chap. 23, 284).
Onomastics: Old High German word for "sword."

SWIFTBROOK the manor Beel offers to Able (I, chap. 50, 317).

SWIT a knight of Duke Marder (II, chap. 11, 126). His device is a gazehound *couchant* (lying down or crouching, but with head up). A gazehound is one that tracks by sight rather than by scent.
Onomastics: Polish word for "dawn, daybreak, sunrise."

SWORD BREAKER Able's sword-like mace, "sort of like a steel bar" (I, glossary). It is a foreign weapon, a mace of the Lothurlings (I, chap. 15, 106). It looks like a sword when sheathed. Named after it broke the captain's sword (I, chap. 20, 129). Later given to Toug (I, chap. 20, 130).

From Stone: "Tau-kien. Chinese weapons with hilts like swords and heavy square metal bars in place of blades. Whether they were used as weapons or for exercise is uncertain, probably the former as some of them are very well finished. Some weigh as much as ten pounds." Figure 778 #4: "Four sided blade with shallow grooves on each side ... length of blade 30.75 inches."

THIAZBOR a giant stronghold owned by Thiazi (II, chap. 8, 88).

THIAZI Gilling's minister and wizard (II, chap. 6, 69). He built the Room of Lost Love in his tower at Utgard.
Myth: (Norse) the giant who stole Idunn and her apples of youth. He was slain by the gods when he chased Loki back into Asgard.

THOAS a duke of Celidon (II, chap. 39, 465).
Myth: (Greek) one of the Greek heroes at the Trojan War.

THOPE Marder's master-at-arms (I, chap. 32, 200). Able jousts with him three times. The knights beat Able, and when Thope tries to stop them, he is stabbed (I, chap. 33, 205). Presumably Thope is stabbed by one of the knights, but Modguda has just said how they hate Agr, Marder's marshal. Woddet says, "Some wretch put his blade into Thope's back" (I, chap. 34, 210). So it is another mysterious stabbing at a melee, like the stabbing of Able in the fight against the Osterling pirates and the stabbing of Gilling.

THORTOWER Arnthor's castle, located in the center of Kingsdoom (II, chap. 28, 348). Princess Morcaine has a tower, and Queen Gaynor has at least a garden, if not a tower of her own. Other locations include the Red Room and Escan's library. The castle also has ancient dungeons that reach down into Aelfrice.

THREE HEARTS AND THREE LIONS the armorer at Forcetti, talking about painting designs on shields, says, "There was one wanted three hearts 'n three lions, all on the one shield. We done it, but it cost the world" (I, chap. 37, 230). This is a reference to a 1961 novel by Poul Anderson, in which Holger Carlsen, a soldier in World War Two, awakens from a head wound in a world of romance as Ogier the Dane. In this alternate world, the evil of faerie is expanding into Europe. The two forces in opposition are Law (Church and humanity) and Chaos (magic and faerie). Holger's girlfriend is a swanmay and Morgan le Fay plays a role.

THRYM captain of Gilling's guards (II, chap. 6, 65). He is the biggest Son of Angr Able ever sees, being twice the height of the tallest man (66). He is in the ambush group (II, chap. 23, 283). Beel kills him (284).
Myth: Norse name meaning "crash," he was the giant who had the hammer in "The Theft of Thor's Hammer" (by an unknown poet). Thrym refused to give it back unless he was given Freyja as his wife. So Thor disguised himself in bridal clothes and went in her place.

THUNOR the Valfather's eldest son, the model for knights (I, chap. 44, 274).
Myth: (Norse) the Old English name for Thor, thunder god of the Æsir.

THUNROLF lord of Round Tower, the garrison at the Mountain of Fire (I, chap. 29, 179). A baron, he wants to prove to Able that a true knight is better than Able, whom he assumes is a fake knight or a Tom O'Bedlam madman. Frustrated that none of his own knights will volunteer to prove this point, he chains himself to Able and enters the Mountain of Fire. After returning to Mythgarthr he offers to adopt Able (I, chap. 31, 193).
Onomastics: The German name "Thun" is a location name for one who lives near a watch tower, or an occupational name for one in charge of a tower; "Rolf" (also German) is "renowned wolf."

THYR "the first peasant girl" (II, glossary; II, chap. 17, 188).
Myth: (Norse) Thyr, "slave girl," is the human wife of demi-god Thrall. Their descendants are the race of thralls (serfs). See LUT.
Commentary: Able mentions Thyr in an exclamation while looking at Utgard, "But oh Thyr and Tyr look at the size of it!" The sense of this seems to be that everyone, from lowly slave to a high god, would surely be impressed by the sight of the giant castle.

TIJANAMIR "prince" title among the Osterlings (II, chap. 37, 442). The six sons of the old Caan are all titled tijanamir, from the Red Tijanamir through to the Black Tijanamir.
Onomastics: possibly "Tijan" (masculine name) plus "emir" (the Arabian title for a military governor).

TIMELINE see HISTORY.

TOM O'BEDLAM an anonymous poem written circa A.D. 1600 about a Bedlamite, a vagrant begging madman. This Tom thinks he is a knight on a fantastic quest for his lady-love, the madwoman Maudlin. The line containing "—and a horse of air," quoted in the text, is from the final stanza:

> With a host of furious fancies
> Whereof I am commander,
> With a burning spear and a horse of air,

To the wilderness I wander.
By a knight of ghosts and shadows
I summoned am to tourney
Ten leagues beyond the wild world's end.
Methinks it is no journey.

The ballad itself has countless versions, and the snippets given in *The Wizard Knight* show variation with the form given above: The line "With a burning spear and a horse of air" becomes "With a lance of prayer and a horse of air," and "Ten leagues beyond the wild world's end" becomes "Ten thousand leagues beyond the moon" (II, chap. 18, 210).

This allusion within the text makes it plain that Able is seen as a Tom O'Bedlam character who is right rather than insane. Indeed, Able has a "horse of air" in his flying mount Cloud, and he commands a host of strange beings: the fire Aelf maidens Baki and Uri, the god dog Gylf, the ogre Org, the witch's cat Mani, and ultimately a few armies of Aelfrice.

TOUG son of OLD TOUG, brother of Ulfa. He is one of the peasant boys who tries to rob Able early on (the other one is Haf). After Able is transformed into a man, he gets Toug to guide him to the outlaws near Glennidam, but they end up going to Aelfrice, where Able leaves Toug with Disiri. Much later, after Able kills the giant Bymir in Jotunland, he meets a mute Toug who guides him to where Eterne is hidden (I, chap. 67, 413). Able requests a boon that Toug put a griffin on his shield. Toug sees Able die. He later uses the knife he finds in Able's saddlebag—probably the dagger Able took from the outlaw cave (I, chap. 14, 100)—lashing it to a pole to form a crude lance.

In the battle against giants, a serving man hits Toug. First the man jumps on Toug's horse behind him and grabs the reins, heading them away. Toug resists and the man hits him on the ear and dumps him (II, chap. 3, 31). Later Toug has to settle with him, presumably with a beating, after Able mentions it (34).

After returning from Skai, Able has Toug heal Baki (II, chap. 4, 42–43). Squire Wistan challenges Toug, frustrated over the non-answers about witch and cat. Toug yields, surrenders Sword Breaker. Wistan says he will drop it down the cistern (II, chap. 15, 174). Baki warns Toug that Beel will give him trouble if he suspects Toug will aid in Baki's quest to get Able to go to Aelfrice (II, chap. 15, 177).

Beel's secret mission for Toug is to go outside the castle and look for giant scaling ladders (II, chap. 16, 183). Toug beats Wistan on his way out.

Toug saves Etela, her mother, and her father Vil. Toug becomes a knight, but as a result of his suffering he is a somewhat reluctant knight. It seems likely that he marries Etela.

Onomastics: Old High German word for "it is useful; be useful." In this sense it is similar to the names Able and Nytir.

TOWER OF GLAS the skyscraper palace Setr built in Aelfrice (I, chap. 22, 140–41). Like a successful Tower of Babel it reaches the next heaven, appearing in Mythgarthr as an equatorial island.

TRISTAN see NAMES ON THE WIND.

TUMBREL "Are you the only man in Mythgarthr who doesn't know the tale of the knight and the tumbrel?" (II, chap. 13, 149). A tumbrel is a two-wheeled cart.

Arthuriana: a reference to Lancelot, who, having lost his horse, hesitates to take the tumbrel. "Does a knight of honor mount the cart of dishonor? Anything must be endured to save the queen." He climbs on and is tagged ever after as "knight of the cart," signifying chivalry and shame.

TUNG a master of arms who taught Garvaon. "Master Tung used to say a true swordsman was a lily blooming in the fire" (I, chap. 55, 342).

Tung-shan (full name Liang-chieh of Tung-shan) was the 9th century founder of Ch'an Buddhism. In systematizing the ranks of awareness between Absolute and Relative reality, he used concrete

metaphors to explain them. Thus, he wrote that in the Fourth Rank of Buddhism, "The master swordsman / Is like the lotus blooming in the fire." Here the lotus is absolute reality and fire is relative reality.
Onomastics: Tung-shan, "East Mountain," is a place in Kowloon, Hong Kong.
Commentary: presumably "lotus" was changed to "lily" because there are no lotuses in the European-like environment of Celidon.

TYR the bravest of the Overcyns (II, chap. 17, 188). See ZIO.
Myth: (Norse) an early war god, later associated with law and justice. In Old Norse Tyr was a synonym for "god," such that Odin bore the title "Sigtyr," the god of victory (Davidson). Tyr was brave enough to feed the wolf Fenrir, and willing to sacrifice his hand in order that the monster could be bound.

U

ULD a farmer who used to live in Griffinsford and had six fingers (I, chap. 3, 34). His house was across from Baldig's.
Onomastics: a variant of *-ulf* (Old Norse *ulfr*), or wolf.

ULFA old Toug's daughter, the girl who makes clothes for Able in Glennidam after he is transformed (I, chap. 8, 60). She is three years older than her brother Toug, but the gap increases during the years he is away in Aelfrice (II, chap. 10, 108). She leaves home to find Able, eventually meeting up with Pouk and camping at the mountain pass. Captured by giants, they end up at Utgard Castle. She marries Pouk. Able secures their freedom and flies Ulfa home to Glennidam on Cloud.
Onomastics: (Icelandic) feminine form of Ulfur, meaning "wolf."

ULFA'S MOTHER she is hiding in the pantry when Able shows up at old Toug's house (I, chap. 8, 62).

UNS a hunchbacked peasant who raised the ogre Org and later joins Able's group. His mother is Nukara and his brother is Duns. His special talent is reading the weather (I, chap. 38, 234). He meets up with Able again at the mountain pass (I, chap. 56, 345). He is stabbed during the fight between Able and Loth (II, chap. 33, 392). Able straightens his hunchback in his healing miracles.
Onomastics: Icelandic word meaning "until," from Old Norse *unz*.

URI a Fire Aelf maiden, friend or sister of Baki (I, chap. 23, 149). Setr makes her Able's slave (150). Uri is the one who swears to serve Able (149). She was a khimaira at the time. She was one of the dancers at the attempt to feed Morcaine to Grengarm.

There is a question of why she did not say Baki needed aid (II, chap. 7, 82) in the episode where Toug ended up healing Baki (II, chap. 4, 41). One possibility is that she feared trouble with Able after the Grengarm episode. Another is that she is serving Able by keeping him away from such a potential trap as healing Baki (either through blood or through Overcyn magic).

Uri tells Able that Baki stabbed Gilling (II, chap. 13, 147).
Onomastics: (Hebrew) a male name meaning "God is my light."

UTGARD Gilling's castle, also the town around it (mentioned I, chap. 61, 372). Where Gylf found Pouk (I, chap. 62, 385). In the castle are Bittergarm, Gilling, Pouk, Schildstarr, Skoel, Thiazi, and Ulfa. In the town are Alca, Gif, Logi, Etela, Lynnet, Rowd, Sceef, and Vil.
Myth: (Norse) a realm outside of Asgard.

UTHOR father of Setr, Morcaine, and Arnthor (II, chap. 33, 395). He had these children by a water dragon of Muspel. Without an heir, Arnthor, the throne would have passed to his brother's line.
Arthuriana: Uther, father of Arthur.

V

VAFTHRUDNIR a giant famous for wisdom (II, chap. 12, 136).
Myth: (Norse) a giant who had dialogue with Odin in the Edda.

VALFATHER, THE king of Skai and the model for kings (I, chap. 11, 80). His wife is Frigg. Thunor is his oldest son, and Lothur is his youngest son. Among his daughters are Idnn and the Lady.

He visits the human Queen Idnn when Uri is about to name the person who attacked King Gilling (II, chap. 20, 234). This makes him a suspect (see MYSTERY OF KING GILLING'S MURDER for details).
Myth: (Norse) Odin, king of the Æsir. From Old High German *wal* ("battlefield, slaughter"), Odin is War-Father, or Norse *valr* ("those slain in battle"). But also a pun on All-Father, a title of Odin.

Odin and his two brothers, Ve (or Lothur) and Vili, created the cosmos and all animate things. Odin gave one of his eyes to Mimir so that he might drink wisdom from his well. See MIRMIR.

VALI a man who helps old Toug in trying to kill Able (I, chap. 8, 64). He wants to take Seaxneat's place as the middleman between outlaws and Glennidam (I, chap. 12, 86).
Myth: (Norse) a son of Odin, or a son of Loki.

VALT Leort's squire, "and a good one" (II, glossary; II, chap. 9, 96).
Onomastics: perhaps from Valter, the Swedish form of Walter "strong fighter," or the Teutonic "powerful ruler."

VE Vali's little boy (I, chap. 8, 65).
Myth: Norse son of Bor and brother of Odin. The name means "giver of feeling." See LOTHUR.

VIDARE one of Marder's knights who beats Able, his comeuppance is a broken nose (I, chap. 34, 214).
Myth: Norse name meaning "tree fighter."

VIL the blind slave who is probably Etela's father (II, chap. 16, 187; chap. 17, 189). She says he is not (II, chap. 17, 195). Prior to his enslavement, he was a conjurer (II, chap. 22, 271). He claims he never touched Etela: he tried to keep her close and safe from the other male slaves, told her he would turn her into a doll. Which is why she is frightened of him (II, chap. 23, 277).
Onomastics: Old Icelandic word for "will, desire, favor," from the Old Norse *vili* ("will"). Note that Vili is, like Lothur, a brother of Odin.
Commentary: the transformation into a doll part echoes an element in *The Book of Knights*. See MEYNARD, YVES.

VIX Thunrolf's body servant, who is there when Thunrolf, Pouk, and Able emerge from the Mountain of Fire one year after they had vanished (I, chap. 31, 192).
Onomastics: German patronymic from a medieval personal name Veit (Latin "Vitus"), i.e., "life."

VOLLA Garvaon's wife, who died giving birth to a boy who also died (I, chap. 57, 355).
Myth: (Norse) a mythic name used in one of the Merseburg charms. Phol and Volla are a brother and sister pair. See PHOLSUNG.

VOLLERLAND a term for Jotunhome found in old books (II, glossary; II, chap. 16, 181).

VORTIGERN see NAMES ON THE WIND.

W

WACE see NAMES ON THE WIND.

WALEWEIN see NAMES ON THE WIND.

WAR WAY the main road from Celidon into Jotunland (I, chap. 43, 269). It connects the mountain pass with Redhall and probably Redhall with Kingsdoom.

WELAND "the man who forged Eterne. He was from Mythgarthr but he became king of the Fire Aelf " (I, glossary). Weland seems to have been the first smith of Mythgarthr, as suggested when Disiri tells Able and Toug, "The first pair of tongs was cast down to fall at the feet of Weland, and with them, a mass of white-hot steel. Six brands Weland made, and six broke. The seventh, Eterne, he could not break" (I, chap. 9, 69).

It seems that Weland went to Alfrice and became king of the Fire

Alf, presumably because of their affinity to fire, the engine of the forge. With regard to his death, an armorer at Forcetti speaks to Able and Pouk, saying, "[the man Weland] was King a' the Fire Aelf... Dragon got him, but people still talk about him" (I, chap. 37, 231).

Late in his reign, King Weland requested aid from Muspel, the level beneath Aelfrice. Help arrived in the form of Setr, who gradually usurped Weland's throne and led two Aelf clans in their war against Kulili.

Talking to Able, Michael of Kleos alludes to Weland's patron, "You should ask whence came the tongs that grasped Eterne " (I, chap. 44, 277). The glossary gives this patron as Zio.

Myth: Anglo-Saxon name of a supernatural smith in the early tradition, known as Volundr in Old Norse poetry. The Norse *Eddas* tell of how Weland and his two elder brothers met three swan maidens by Wolf Lake. For seven (or nine) years they lived in love together, but then one day the women flew away, since they were Valkyries. The elder brothers sought their lost loves, each following a different path, but Weland stayed by the lake. Nidud, a rival king, captured Weland, claiming the smith had stolen his gold. As punishment he cut Weland's sinews and moved his forge to a remote island. The smith had his revenge by killing Nidud's two sons and seducing his daughter. Some versions then have him escaping to Alfheim where he lived and worked a long time.

Weland fashioned the mail shirt worn by Beowulf (*Beowulf,* lines 450-55), and forged the magic sword Gram (Old Norse "wrath"). Nidud repeatedly calls Weland "Lord of the Alf." For additional links to Weland see ALVIT (Weland's wife) and EGIL (Weland's elder brother).

WER a villager who joined Berthold the Black in singing to the Overcyns when the demon was pressing (II, chap. 22, 264).

Onomastics: wer is an archaic term for "a man."

Myth: (Akkadian) a storm god. A minor deity, his attendant is Humbaba, the fierce guardian of the forest.

WESTERN TRADER the ship Able takes from Irringsmouth (I, chap. 15, 101). It trades up and down the coast of Celidon and goes west to the islands between Celidon and the land of the Lothurlings.

WHITE TI|ANAMIR the old Caan's third son, whose fate foretold was that he would reign but die young at the hands of his followers. He became caan at the death of the Brown Caan. Less than an hour later he was sorely wounded. Unable to even kill himself, he begged his friends, and they obliged (II, chap. 37, 443).

WILIGA Escan's lover (II, chap. 36, 432). She was his mother's maid and she died giving birth to his bastard, Payn.
Onomastics: Old English word for basket; but in Grimm's *Teutonic Mythology, wiliga* is a conversion of Old Frisian *wigila*, "sorcery, witchcraft" (1033).

WISTAN Garvaon's squire (II, chap. 12, 130). He is nearly 18 years old (II, chap. 33, 393) and has two sisters (II, chap. 30, 362). At Utgard he challenges Toug on the stairs and takes Sword Breaker when Toug yields (II, chap. 15, 174). He claims he will drop it down the cistern. He comes up with the idea of getting Org to confess to killing King Gilling (II, chap. 25, 309), even if Org has not really done it (311).

After Garvaon dies, Wistan is Able's squire, and he argues with Toug and Uns, trying to establish the pecking order. Able dismisses him when he runs from the library at the sight of a ghost (II, chap. 29, 354). But then Wistan declares he wants to be a knight like Able, and he takes him back (362). Able gives him Loth's sword (II, chap. 32, 390-91).

He does some scouting before the River Battle (II, chap. 39, 465).
Onomastics: Saint Wystan (Wigstan) died in A.D. 840.

WITH A LANCE AND A PRAYER and a horse of air" (II, chap. 18, 210). This is a line from Tom O'Bedlam, which see.

WIZARD KNIGHT, THE (EXCERPT) the story first appeared in *Conjunctions: 39 "The New Wave Fabulists" Issue* (2002) as a selection of five chapters.

- The Ruined Town (chap. 2)
- Spiny Orange (chap. 3)
- Sir Ravd (chap. 4)
- Terrible Eyes (chap. 5)
- Disiri (chap. 6)

WODDET the biggest knight at Sheerwall (I, chap. 33, 205), and just about the only friend Able makes there (I, glossary). He refuses to participate when the knights are mobbing Able. His device is a menhir with a spear through it (II, chap. 11, 126). He is in the campaign that kills the old Caan (II, chap. 37, 443). He is also in the Battle of the Five Fates. He is the second knight to challenge Able at the pass, where he is disguised as the Knight of the Sun, wearing golden armor and a shield with a gold sun. Hela the half-giant girl falls in love with him and he seems to reciprocate. Later he is chosen as the second champion in the three fights against Smiler's Dragon Warriors (II, chap. 38, 454). He loses to Ironmouth, but survives.
Onomastics: perhaps *wod-* of the German "Wodin," in a pet form, i.e., "little Odin," suggesting berserker madness in battle.

WOLF a list of wolves in the text includes Fenrir, Geri, Hrolfr, nornhound, Skoll, Thunrolf, Uld, Ulfa, and Wulfkill.

WULFKIL a creek that empties into the Griffin where Able, Ravd, and Svon camp the first night (I, chap. 4, 38).

WYT a sailor on the *Western Trader* (I, chap. 20, 127).
Onomastics: Old English for word "wise" and a Frisian word meaning "white"; close to the English name Wyth, "from the willow tree."

Y

YCER king of the Ice Aelf (II, chap. 33, 396). The leader of an Aelf clan that resisted Setr's attempt at taking over Aelfrice, he is in league with Disiri and Brunman.

YENS a little port between Forcetti and Kingsdoom (I, chap. 20, 127).

YMIR the first giant (II, chap. 4, 46).
Myth: (Norse) primeval giant from whose body the world was formed.

YOND Woddet's squire, who throws himself down on Able when the others are trying to kill him at Sheerwall Castle. Later he scouts with Wistan before the River Battle (II, chap. 39, 465).
Onomastics: the common use of the Middle English word *yond* is to designate something in the middle distance, i.e., *yonder*. But Scott Wowra notes that in *The Faerie Queene,* Spenser used it in a different way that still causes argument among scholars, some of whom say

it means "furious, transported with rage." In Spenser's poem, this applies to Sir Guyon, who twice in book II (cantos ii and iv) tries to stop a battle between two knights, only to get embroiled in the fighting himself. So Wolfe's Yond seems to be the Guyon that Sir Guyon tries to be.

YVAIN see NAMES ON THE WIND.

Z

ZIO "the Overcyn who helped Weland. He has a lot of names" (II, glossary only).
Myth: (Norse) another name for Tyr.

THE WIZARD KNIGHT SYNOPSIS

THE KNIGHT

The narrator begins the letter to his brother Ben, telling how he cut off a branch of spiny orange and walked from America to Mythgarthr and then to Aelfrice, only to wake up in Parka's cave at the edge of Mythgarthr. She tells him his name is Able (1). He goes to Bluestone Island, and when he drinks some rainwater he sees a phantom knight for a moment. Then he joins some fishermen. The next day he goes looking for Griffinsford and finds Bold Berthold's hut (2). Two days later they set out for the ruins of Griffinsford, where Berthold tells him about the place (3).

Able lives with Berthold for one spring. One summer day he meets Sir Ravd and Squire Svon, who are trying to restore order to the ravaged and lawless land. Squire Svon picks a fight and Able beats him (4). Svon comes back from the forest with a message from the Aelf (5).

They arrive at Glennidam where Ravd interviews the villagers one at a time. Ravd sends Able to find Seaxneat or his wife Disira (6).

Able calls for Disira but gets Disiri instead. In exchange for one drop of his blood she makes him into a man (7).

As a naked man Able returns to Glennidam at twilight the next day and strikes down old Toug for laughing at him. He gets Ulfa to sew him some clothes. Then he interrupts the ambush and takes young Toug out toward the outlaw camp (8). But they slip into Aelfrice where they meet with Disiri. She tells Able he must get the sword Eterne. She borrows Toug. Able sleeps in Aelfrice but wakes up in Mythgarthr. Calling for Disiri, he finds Disira instead. Days had passed during his brief time away. He takes Disira to Bold Berthold's hut (9).

Able has Disira and her baby stay with them for weeks but then they prepare for her return to Glennidam before winter arrives. On the day Able sees his first giant, Seaxneat raids the hut, leaving Disira dead, baby Ossar left to die, and Berthold missing, presumed dead. Able buries Disira and carries Ossar toward Glennidam (10). On the way there he meets some Bodachan who give him Gylf and take Ossar (11).

At Glennidam Able questions Toug's family, then allows old Toug to join him in going to the outlaw cave about an hour away (12). They make their way to the cave (13) and have a big battle with the outlaws. After it is over, Able finds Ravd's broken sword, proof that he had died there (14).

After dividing up the loot, Able goes to Irringsmouth to buy passage to Forcetti. He meets Pouk. He buys an unusual mace (15). Able uses unnecessary roughness in renting the captain's quarters (16). The next day the ship is loaded with cargo (17). Pouk makes it a steady job by staying with Able. Gylf is hiding in the hold. On the second day the ship puts out (18).

They have a big fight against Osterling pirates. Able is stabbed in the side and lies below decks for many days (19). Though he is badly wounded, he takes Gylf to confront the captain in his cabin. The captain starts to fight and they kill him (20).

Concerned about his wound, Able asks Gylf to fetch Aelf to heal him. The dog goes and some Sea Aelf come along with Garsecg. They take him to Aelfrice through the sea (21). Garsecg has the ocean heal Able, then teaches Able to summon the ocean force within him. They approach the Tower of Glas (22). As they go up the stairs they are attacked by khimairae. Garsecg turns into a dragon and five khimairae pick up Able and fly high. He manages to hold two as the others let go, and he lands hard on the stairs. These two are Baki and Uri, who become his slaves. Garsecg wants Able to select a weapon from the vast armory, but Able refuses all but Eterne, which is not available (23).

After days of climbing they emerge on the Isle of Glas in Mythgarthr. Able finds the goblet, the bones, and the glass tube (24). He learns the bones are those of a woman. He talks with Garsecg about the Osterling pirates (25). Garsecg examines the scroll from the tube. It is written in Celidonian script, which Able cannot read. On the way to the beach, Garsecg shows Able his true feathered-snake form (26).

Garsecg shows him a pool that is a portal to Aelfrice. Thinking of Disiri, Able dives in. He meets Kulili (27). When he swims back up he is in the sea, and the *Western Trader* is nearby. He boards, meets Pouk, and learns he was gone three years. Sailing north toward Forcetti, the ship puts in at the little port near the Mountain of Fire (28).

Able and Pouk go up the mountain to the garrison. Because of irregularities, Able is compelled to engage in mock combat. He loses gracefully (29). Then Lord Thunrolf closes his trap and has Pouk chained by the ankle to a large stone he can barely carry. Thunrolf pushes Pouk into the volcano. Able wants to rescue him and Thunrolf, wanting to prove the worth of a knight versus a pretender, asks for a volunteer to go with him. No knight volunteers. In disgust Thunrolf handcuffs himself to Able and they begin the descent. Thunrolf fails to best Able. They rescue Pouk from a dragon Garsecg in Muspel (30).

When the three emerge back up on Mythgarthr, they find a year has passed since they left. After a month or two of rest, Able and Pouk catch a ride on the *Western Trader* again (31).

At Sheerwall near Forcetti, Able tries to seek service with Duke

Marder. He practices jousting a few times then is jumped by the knights for a cutting reply (32).

He wakes up in a bed in the tower of Master Agr. Maid Modguda tells him how Thope was stabbed trying to break up the fight. At night Uri and Baki find him. Baki has him drink her blood for rapid healing (33). The next day Able meets Woddet, then Duke Marder, who gives him the quest to prove himself: holding a mountain pass until there is ice in the harbor (34).

On the way to the inn, Able and Pouk stop at a farm that has a ghost problem. Able promises to stop by on their way back (35).

At the inn, Able argues over the bill. Sir Nytir ambushes them on their way out. Able wins, and Nytir tries treachery. Able wins again. He pays a reduced bill (36).

They go to an armorer to adjust his newly won mail and shield. A storm comes and they stop at the farmhouse (37). At dinner Able hears wind in the chimney and goes outside alone to meet Disiri. He is too slow. He meets Baki, sends her to watch the house, and calls Gylf (38). Gylf comes around, and so does Uri (39). Able arranges to wrestle against Org the ogre (40). Able wrestles Org and loses, but wins when Gylf, Baki, and Uri overpower Org. Then Org wants to serve Able. Uns has run off. Able and Pouk take Org to Sheerwall Castle with them (41).

The next morning, Able tries to meet with Caspar the Chief Warder but causes an incident at breakfast (42). The solution is for Able to take Org and hold a mountain pass. But his new squire Svon is difficult in the forest, so Able leaves him to avoid killing him (43). During his quiet time he meets Michael, a man from Kleos, who is on his way to find Able in Aelfrice (44). After Michael leaves, Able builds an altar and sacrifices to the gods of Kleos.

Able and Gylf move to try and catch up with Pouk, who they learn had also moved away from Svon and is heading toward the pass. The man and his dog find shelter in a witch's cottage (45) where they meet a talking cat named Mani, the deceased witch's familiar (46).

The trio catches up with Lord Beel's group where Able hopes to borrow a horse (47). Able meets Beel and Princess Idnn and becomes impressed into their service until they reach the pass (48). They have their first battle with the half-giants, the "Mice" (49). Beel proposes an archery contest between Able and Garvaon, but he asks Able who told Idnn about the carnage on the cliff. It was Mani, but Able cannot tell him that (50).

Able has a dream of being a child on the Griffin River. When he wakes he talks to Mani and confirms that Mani told Idnn. The archery contest begins (51). Able's arrows cause supernatural effects. He leaves in a rush. Gylf finds him later in the dark and leads him back to the camp (52).

At breakfast Garvaon talks to Able. Able uses his boon by asking Garvaon to teach him swordcraft (53). Able is riding at the front of the line to spot ambushers when Idnn rides up to chat. She talks about her fate as bride for the giant king, and how she had hoped that Able would save her (54). Garvaon teaches swordcraft to Able (55).

Uns catches up with Able. Able reaches the pass and finds evidence that Pouk had camped there, fought, and left to go further into Jotunland (56). Garvaon gives a second lesson, this time about foining, then asks Able to not be his rival for Idnn (57, 58). Beel tries a magic spell to find the fate of Pouk. Giants attack the camp in their absence (59).

Beel's knights train all the servants and maids to fight, and the entire party pursues the giants for the loot they had stolen (61). Able, riding ahead, has dreams and meets up with Gylf, Uri, and Baki. Gylf tells him Pouk is in Utgard (62).

Able, Gylf, and the Aelfmaidens harass the giants by stealing their mules. Able talks to Gylf about his ability to change size (63). They surprise an old lady in the hedgerow who was on her way to meet a friend (64). She is Gerda and her friend is Bold Berthold (65). Able promises to rescue them both on his way back from Utgard (66).

A giant catches Able sleeping in his barn. Able kills him in the kitchen. Then he hears the wind in the chimney. He rushes out to find Disiri and hears the many names on the wind. He finds Toug, but Toug cannot speak. Together they look for Disiri (67).

They end up at the Grotto of the Griffin, source of the river. It looks dangerous. Able sleeps and dreams. Then he questions Toug and learns that Toug will be able to speak when Able gets Eterne. Able goes into the cave. He finds an altar and calls out. Nothing happens. He dives down into the wellspring of the Griffin to retrieve his lost boots and mail. Through repeated efforts he manages to get a different suit of mail and a sword.

The dragon's head erupts from the well. It is Grengarm, and some Aelf (Uri among them) are making a human sacrifice to him. Able draws the sword he has just found: it is Eterne (68).

Able fights the dragon and Aelfs, supported by the phantom knights of the sword. The dragon escapes. Able saves the woman, but then she disappears.

Able goes outside and with Toug rides the animal Griffin in pursuit of Grengarm. They harry the dragon and Able kills him. Then Able is caught up by Alvit the valkyrie (69).

THE WIZARD

Uns and Toug tell Lord Beel and Princess Idnn of Sir Able's death. They are all preparing to face giants. Mani talks to Toug (1).

Svon rides up and insults Toug, so Toug sucker-punches him with the butt of his crude lance, breaking Svon's nose. Svon tells how Org is following him. Together they find the giant's farm where blinded Bold Berthold awaits the return of Sir Able (2). They take Berthold to Beel, and he tells of the giants eating there. They move to get the pack animals and fight the giants on horseback. In the middle of battle a serving man is riding in the saddle with Toug. He knocks Toug out. When Toug wakes up, on foot, the battle is still going on, now with bows. Toug takes a fallen giant's knife as a sword. Then Sir Able appears in green and gold.

After the battle, Able teaches Toug how to care for his horse (3).

Baki is near death and begs Able to save her with a sacrifice of his blood. He refuses, but he tells Toug how to do it (4). Afterwards when they sleep, Toug and Able visit Dream, next door on the fourth level. When awake, Able knights Svon and Toug becomes Svon's squire. Able leaves to hold the pass as he had promised. Idnn has a private interview with Squire Toug to ask about Sir Svon, with whom she is romantically interested (5).

The party led by Beel arrives at Utgard. Thrym the guard giant says his king wants Idnn's cat Mani. Toug is sent ahead with Mani (6).

Meanwhile Able's party is heading to the pass to fulfill his quest. Gerda's half-giant children Hela and Heimir join them (7).

Thiazi, prime minister of King Gilling, questions Toug and Mani. Then Mani goes out the tower window and climbs down to another window. Toug and Baki follow, searching for Mani and Ulfa, Toug's sister (8).

The Knight of Leopards faces Able at the pass (9).

Toug finds Ulfa. She tells him to look for her husband, Pouk. Toug, Ulfa, and Baki swear an oath to help each other: to help Ulfa and Pouk escape; to help Toug be a knight like Able; to help Baki bring Able to Aelfrice to kill Setr. Mani then tells them King Gilling wants Able to conquer Celidon for him (10).

The Knight of the Sun faces Able at the pass (11).

Lord Beel and party are formally presented to King Gilling. Gilling proposes a combat between giants and knights. In the confused melee, Gilling is struck a major wound by an unknown assailant. A hasty wedding is arranged for Gilling and Idnn (12).

Uri visits Able at the pass. Then Idnn comes from the giant side, now a queen. The Black Knight challenges Able (13).

Back at Utgard, Huld (Mani's ghost witch owner) tells Toug how she has played as a false Idnn to allow the real one to ride out for Able.

Idnn tells Able and his group about the wounding of Gilling. They puzzle over the mystery of who did it. They arrange things so that Able can leave the pass with his honor intact and the party can go to Utgard (14).

At Utgard, Schildstarr argues with Thiazi. Squire Wistan tries to question Squire Toug about voices, then grows belligerent at his evasive answers. Wistan takes Sword Breaker from him. Gilling's wound starts bleeding again (15). Schildstarr announces to the crowd that his faction is guarding the king. Beel tells Toug he has a secret mission for him.

With Able's group, Idnn tells him about giantesses. After the rest of the camp is asleep, Able rides Cloud through the sky to Utgard.

Beel's mission is for Toug to search the giant village for siege ladders. On his way out on this deadly task he meets and beats Wistan. Out on the street he stops Org from eating a girl, Etela, who tells him about the siege tools she knows of (16). She takes him to the place where she lives, where the tools are being forged. He meets Vil. Uri shows up. Toug meets Etela's mother. The giant master Logi wakes up and charges Toug, but Org helps Toug kill Logi.

Toug takes Etela to the castle, where Able has already arrived. They meet at the sickbed of Gilling (17). Then they meet with Schildstarr about action to take on the tools. Able returns Ulfa to Glennidam, and hears the wind in the chimney. He rushes out to meet Disiri. Then he rides back to camp, sobered (18). Mani had been hiding in the saddlebag, so he is now reunited with Queen Idnn at the camp. He tells her that Beel is trying to get Toug killed.

At Utgard, Schildstarr is sent out to buy the forge and its tools. Svon and Toug are sent out to buy food and to bring Logi's slaves back to the castle.

Mani tells Able about the Room of Lost Love.

Svon tells Toug about Ravd and how their own mission is like the one that killed Ravd (19).

Uri visits Idnn. Uri is on the verge of naming the one who stabbed Gilling when the Valfather enters the pavilion. He urges Idnn to help Able regain his only love.

Svon and Toug set out.

Able asks Mani about the Room of Lost Love.

Toug kills a giant at the forge. Svon and Toug find an auction going on, where Schildstarr is buying up most of the items. Svon takes possession of the slaves in the king's name. They buy food at the market but a giant starts trouble so Svon kills him and they all hurry to the castle. The fighting escalates. Queen Idnn appears and orders them to stop. In the courtyard the body of a dead Frost Giant is King Gilling (20).

Able bargains with Thiazi, discussing the murder of Gilling. Thiazi allows him to go into the Room of Lost Love if he takes Etela's mother Lynnet with him (21). They enter the room and find Goldenlawn, Lynnet's home. Mani sneaks in, too. Then Able finds his way to Parka's grotto, and from there he swims to the Isle of Glas where he meets Mag, mother of the real Able and Bold Berthold. Now he finds he can read her scroll.

After they come out of the room, Pouk comes to tell them Schildstarr has declared himself king. Lynnet, now somewhat recovered, asks Able if he will be her new husband. He declines the offer (22). Vil performs his conjuring tricks for Able. Mani confesses what he saw in the Room of Lost Love.

Hela shows the Duke's party the giants' ambush and in the fighting Able's party from Utgard arrives to help (23). The next day the group heads south into unseasonably warm weather. At the evening camp Idnn convinces Able to take her with him in flying to scout behind. They find the enemy camp and return to their own (24).

The next morning has a thick fog. Toug and others become lost in it. Able sets out to find them (25). Uri shows up and they are in Aelfrice. They go to the beach where a large white dragon stands out in the water: Kulili. Then Able sees the Tower of Glas, and at the isle on top he sees Toug and the others.

Down on the beach Garsecg meets them. Garsecg tells his version of things. Then Able goes into the sea to fight Kulili.

After dealing with Kulili, Able swims to the Tower of Glas where Toug had fought his way down. They meet up with Svon and Garvaon. Able sets up the fight of Garsecg/Setr versus Svon and Garvaon. Able tells how he yielded to Kulili and Setr strikes at Svon. Setr kills Garvaon but is throttled by Vil who is using Able's magic bowstring that he had stolen. Garvaon seemingly confesses to killing Gilling, and dies. A Valkyrie gathers him up (26).

Able and party return to camp in Jotunland, where they bury Garvaon. They fight their way out of the mountains. Able has to explain why he wouldn't fight Setr. Later the ghost Mag talks to Able through Lynnet. The party continues south. Able rides ahead to Redhall, his new manor, stopping first at Goldenlawn in the same area. At Redhall he hears the wind in the chimney and runs out to see Disiri, seemingly over at Goldenlawn's garden grotto (27). Morcaine magically visits him at Redhall, reminding him that he rescued her at the grotto of the Griffin. Wistan, Pouk, and Uns arrive bearing his loot from Jotunland, including a magic helm. Uri comes by but she flees when Able asks her about the helm (28).

The group travels south for more than a week to reach Kingsdoom. Able and Wistan ride to the castle Thortower the next day and meet with Escan the Earl Marshall (29). Able tries the helm and sees different forms of Uri and Gylf.

Able performs well at the mounted archery contest but his borrowed bowstring breaks and he does not dine with King Arnthor. Still, Queen Gaynor chooses him as her champion (30). Morcaine says she will help him meet her brother. Able wins three matches and expects to be invited to the king's table, but the invitation does not come. Escan invites Able to stay at the castle and begins bargaining with him (31). Escan deduces that the secret message Able carries is from Disiri. Escan admits his dream is to visit Aelfrice, and Able agrees to take him after the message is delivered.

Able is Gaynor's champion in a trial by combat. Morcaine's champion is a reanimated dead knight. Able triumphs and at last is invited to the king's table (32). At the dinner the message starts coming out of Able. Accusing Able of treason, Arnthor takes Eterne and has Able thrown into the dungeon (33). Uri visits, then Morcaine. Uri gives him an Ice Aelf sword that was hidden away (34).

Time passes. Arnthor leads an army against the Osterlings. The Queens Gaynor and Idnn consult Able about shoring up the defenses of Kingsdoom. He bends his parole, for which he is chained at the dungeon's twelfth level. After weeks Arnthor returns and releases him. Able takes Escan on a trip to Aelfrice, and then to realms below (35).

They are gone for half a day but return to find Kingsdoom in ruins under Osterling occupation. With Uns and a beggar woman they head for Sevengates. Disiri meets Able and tells him of his friends holding out at Redhall. They go there and wipe out the Osterling besiegers, but Able betrays his oath to the Valfather by doing some weather magic, and so loses his magical mount Cloud (36).

Able leads a group south to aid the king, passing through the ruins of Irringsmouth, Forcetti, and Kingsdoom on the way to the Mountain of Fire. Arnthor is wounded, resting in bed. Able learns about the sword destined to kill the Black Caan. Then the king's forces abandon the hard-won mountain.

Morcaine tries to tempt Able into becoming king by marrying her. She introduces him to Lothur, who proposes a deal of three wishes granted for Able breaking his oath three more times (37).

Queen Gaynor visits Able and tries to tempt him into becoming king by marrying her. He forestalls.

Ten days later they meet Smiler with his five hundred Dragon Warriors and engage in a deadly contest. Able seems to die in the first set, Woddet falls in the second set, and Kei dies in the third set. Yet Able flies Cloud to snatch Smiler, taking him to meet Lothur (who presumably tells the dragon warriors to join with Able against the Osterlings, to gain a kingdom for themselves).

The ghost Mag talks through Lynnet to Bold Berthold and Able (38).

They meet the Osterlings in a series of battles. Preparing for the final battle, Able promises a thousand Aelf archers. Arnthor gives Eterne back to Able and Able gives him the sword fated to kill the Black Caan (39).

At the River Battle, Able fights a dragon and then summons the Aelf archers as a god. Arnthor meets the Black Caan at the water and triumphs over him yet dies shortly thereafter.

After the battle, Able breaks his oath and heals wounded Bold Berthold and many others. Valfather comes and invites him to return to Skai. Instead Able sacrifices his Overcyn-infused blood to Disiri, sealing his fate (40).

BIBLIOGRAPHY

Davidson, Hilda Roderick Ellis. *Scandinavian Mythology.* London: Penguin Books, 1964.

Ellis, Peter Berresford. *Dictionary of Celtic Mythology.* Santa Barbara: ABC-CLIO, c1992.

Lacy, Norris J. *The New Arthurian Encyclopedia.* New York: Garland Publishing, 1991.

Lindow, John. *Handbook of Norse Myth.* Santa Barbara: ABC-CLIO, c2001.

Monaghan, Patricia. *The Encyclopedia of Celtic Mythology and Folklore.* New York: Facts on File, Inc., 2004.

Orchard, Andy. *Dictionary of Norse Myth and Legend.* London: Cassell, 1998.

Rose, Carol. *Giants, Monsters, and Dragons.* New York: W.W. Norton & Co., 2001.

Stone, George Cameron. *A Glossary of the Construction, Decoration and Use of Arms and Armor: In All Countries and in All Times.* New York: Jack Brussel, 1961.

Sturluson, Snorri. *The Prose Edda.* Translated by Jean I. Young. Berkeley: University of California Press, 1973.

Printed in Great Britain
by Amazon